D0284183

It Turns
Out
Like
This

44944359

It Turns Out Like This

A Novel in Stories

stephen coyne

Many Voices Project #134

East Baton Rouge Parish Library
Baton Rouge, Louisiana

©2016 by Stephen Coyne
First Edition
Library of Congress Control Number: 2015953393
ISBN: 978-0-89823-344-5
eISBN: 978-0-89823-345-2

Cover and interior design by Kristin Clarys
Author photo by Shane Monahan Photography

The publication of *It Turns Out Like This* is made possible by the generous support of Minnesota State University Moorhead, The McKnight Foundation, the Dawson Family Endowment, and other generous contributors to New Rivers Press.

MINNESOTA STATE UNIVERSITY MOORHEAD.   THE McKNIGHT FOUNDATION

For copyright permission, please contact Frederick T. Courtright at 570-839-7447 or permdude@eclipse.net.

New Rivers Press is a nonprofit literary press associated with Minnesota State University Moorhead.

Alan Davis, Director and Senior Editor
Nayt Rundquist, Managing Editor
Kevin Carollo, MVP Poetry Coordinator
Bayard Godsave, MVP Prose Coordinator
Thom Tammaro, Poetry Editor
Thomas Anstadt, Co-Art Director
Trista Conzemius, Co-Art Director
Wayne Gudmundson, Consultant
Suzzanne Kelley, Consultant

Publishing Interns:
Laura Grimm, Anna Landsverk, Desiree Miller, Mikaila Norman

It Turns Out Like This book team:
Sarah Bosak, Taylor Brown, Sheena Norstedt, Morgan Tuscherer

∞ Printed in the USA on acid-free, archival-grade paper.

It Turns Out Like This is distributed nationally by Small Press Distribution.

New Rivers Press
c/o MSUM
1104 7th Avenue South
Moorhead, MN 56563
www.newriverspress.com

The kid looks to me
for comfort I cannot find,
and my wife hopes I can live
being not enough, forever.

For Lynne

Contents

Ice Boy

Stu Jakes heard her drive up, but he didn't pull his head out of the icemaker just to get a look at the Wiggler. He'd seen it all before—the short shorts, the halter top, the come-ons. No, it was a hundred and one degrees at the Boat Basin Marina. A hot wind had blown everybody off the water, and Stu was happy to keep his head in the machine. He could see his breath in there. Furry hoods framed the Eskimo Boys' friendly, round faces. He filled a dozen bags with ice and twisted them closed. The Eskimo Boys flashed big smiles. Stu stacked them in the wheelbarrow so they all faced the same way. The Boys smiled and waved. They didn't care about a single thing.

He shoved and cussed the wheelbarrow out onto the porch where the Wiggler stood, hand-on-hip, next to the chest freezer. She was a speed freak and a whore. Everybody at the Basin knew that. Usually she aimed herself at bikers or cops because, as far as her nose cared, they had what she needed. But now she wanted something from Bo, who ran the Basin, and so she was giving her little show for the guys there on the porch.

"Anybody know," she said, "where Rickie's at?"

"Gone," Bo said. "Couple hours ago."

The Wiggler clicked her tongue. She switched hips. "Where?"

"Augustine Beach is what he told us."

"Well," she said. "Who wants to take me?" Her eyes flashed, and she turned from face to face. "Hmm?" she said. "Who?"

Bo looked at Lefty and smiled. They were both doing the math— what it would cost and what they would get. Their speedboats burned a hundred dollars of gas an hour. But the real cost of a ride with the Wiggler would be their marriages, their peace of mind. Bo flicked his cigarette into the boatyard. "Too windy," he said.

"That's it?" she said. "Wind?"

Bo dug the wallet from his pocket and pulled out his boat's registration card. "See there?" He showed it to the Wiggler. "It says 'pleasure craft.' It don't say 'asswupper.'"

"What you need," Lefty said, "is a workboat."

"Ahh," Bo said. "That's right. Workboat's made for rough weather, ain't that right, Stew Beef?"

Stu opened the chest freezer. He lifted a bag from the wheelbarrow and sank it into the cold fog. He knew what Bo was trying to do—throw the girl with too much past in with the geezer who didn't have enough.

Stu lived in an old crabbing boat that had no name, only the numbers 247 painted free-hand on the sides of the cabin. He did odd jobs around the Basin to pay for his slip. He crabbed. He eeled. But beyond those things, they didn't know much about Stu.

Not that there was much to know—a daughter, Gloria, had gone over to her mother's side in the divorce. She was probably twenty-four or -five by now. She'd had a baby too, but Stu only heard about that fourth hand. He didn't even know if it was a boy or a girl. No, his daughter had followed the money into her mother's second marriage.

And nobody at the Basin knew about his old boss, either. For twenty years, he had promised to set Stu up in business. But when Pressy died, there was no will and no provision for Stu. The business turned out to be mostly debt, anyway, and Pressy's niece planned to sell the land, the salvage yard, the dredge—everything. Stu was living on 247 by then. The boat had never been titled, and so four days before the sale, he started the motor and simply powered away from Pressy's place.

Now here he was, a water hermit doing odd jobs during the day and drinking rum at night to keep down the dreams. On a good morning, his day dawned without memories. He'd sit on the edge of his coffin-berth and boil up a pot of coffee there in the tiny cabin. No wife, no daughter, no dreams, no problems.

"This wind ain't nothing," Bo said, "for that boat of yours, is it, Beef?"

Stu turned from the freezer and gave them the Eskimo smile. It was friendly and meant nothing.

"Fifty dollars," Bo said, "if you take this young lady across the bay and bring me back a case of that Blue Crab beer they sell over there."

The case would cost twenty-five or thirty dollars, Stu figured. That left twenty for his time and trouble. "Tank of diesel?" he said.

"This is a damned damsel in distress, Beef. How can you worry about diesel?"

Stu shrugged. Water dripped from the wheelbarrow.

"Alright," Bo said. "Five gallons of diesel and fifty dollars. When I get the beer, you get the money."

Stu put the rest of the bags in the freezer. He closed the lid and a puff of cold air fell on his feet. He turned to the Wiggler.

Her eyes were a washed-out blue, and the sun had bleached her eyebrows so blonde that they were almost clear. The story at the Basin was that her ex had friends on the police force, and after the divorce, they kept pulling her over. It was only a matter of time before they found drugs. That cost her custody of their kid. And after a while, when she started to date again, her boyfriends always seemed to get caught with drugs, too. That was the way it went for the Wiggler until she found Rickie. Bikers, it turned out, could take care of themselves. It was a deal with darkness, but that was the offer life made her.

"Ready?" Stu asked.

The Wiggler flashed a smile. "Always."

Stu led the way across the yard and out to the last run of slips. Most of the boats were slick fiberglass, but 247 was a grubby wooden thing that smelled like diesel fuel and dead fish. Bo made Stu keep it in the last run where the slips were mainly mud at low tide. That was fine with Stu. Using what nobody else wanted had become his personal method of being rich.

Fiddler crabs ducked into their mud holes when Stu walked by. The Wiggler narrowed her eyes when she saw the boat, but she didn't flinch. She stepped over the gunwale and in. Stu started the motor, and the Wiggler helped him untie the lines. After a stop at the fuel dock, he powered out of the Basin and turned toward the salt breeze.

The Wiggler disappeared into the little cabin. It was all the home Stu had, and he did not like her being in there. But she was out in a flash—naked, a towel hanging from her hand. She had once been pretty, but her knees were too big now, and her hips were just points. She looked at him as if to say, "Want?"

But Stu did not want. He gave her the Eskimo smile. The secret was not wanting.

She shrugged and climbed onto the cabin top to sunbathe. 247 swung right as it climbed the waves and then left on the way down. Stu sat back in the captain's seat, one finger on the wheel, and let the boat wallow its way across the bay. Off in the distance, he caught glimpses of his line of crab traps, the buoys rising and falling.

Half an hour later, they were motoring through the anchorage at Augustine Beach. The Wiggler had put her skimpy clothes back on and was looking through Stu's binoculars. "I don't see his boat," she said.

When they got close to the dock, she showed good boat-sense—not trying to tie up until Stu had backed to a stop. She cleated off. Stu watched her do the figure eight and turn the hitch.

The Wiggler saw him looking. She stood up and winked. "Come on," she said. "Keep me company. We'll go home in a while."

"I've got to get a case of that beer, anyhow," he said.

She gave a little laugh at that, and they walked together across the beach and up the wooden steps of the Bayview Bar, where the long front porch smelled of piss and stale beer.

The Wiggler threw extra action into her walk as she approached the large man in denim on a stool outside the front door. "Hey, Bang," she said. It was the same come-on that she tried with Bo. "Where's Rickie?"

Bang's lips disappeared into his toothless smile. "What side of the street you working today, cop-fucker?"

The Wiggler edged toward Bang and put a hand on his knee. "Where I get what I need," she cooed.

Bang shifted his stare to Stu.

"He's okay," the Wiggler said. "Seen Rickie?"

Stu thought he could walk in, but Bang blocked the door. He stared over Stu's head. "You ain't a biker," he said, "so this ain't a bar."

Now Bo's game was clear—send old half-ghost Stu Beef with the Wiggler as his date to buy un-buyable beer from bikers. It was bound to make a story worth the five gallons of diesel fuel.

Stu turned away and drifted down the porch. He stood at the long railing and watched 247 rocking at the dock. The bay was four miles across right there, and rising from the marshes on the far side was the nuclear plant, huge and all out of proportion to the landscape. Even miles away, it loomed over the Bayview's porch like some comic book image. The Wiggler came up beside Stu. She dragged her hand on the railing and sighed. She sat on one of the old kitchen chairs. Her foot tapped. She crossed and re-crossed her legs. She sighed again and looked at her wrist for the watch that wasn't there.

"I don't know," the Wiggler said. "Rickie usually scores for me. These guys." She sucked her lower lip. "They can be hard to deal with." She stood up and joined Stu at the railing. "You got a cigarette?"

"No," Stu said.

She turned and faced him. "Got anything else?"

The hot wind had dried Stu's sweat, and he could feel the crust of salt when he wrinkled his forehead. "Maybe I should go see about drinks," he said.

"No." The Wiggler turned away and looked out over the water. "I'll do it," she said. She took a breath, and when she let it out again, something in her left along with it. She folded her arms across her chest and made her way back to the door. Whatever she said to Bang turned his smile into a sinkhole. He motioned her into the bar.

Stu heard a sound, part laugh, part scream. He started for the door, but two bikers came out and turned him back toward the railing.

Stu stood there, bookended, and frowned out at the bay.

Hoots and another ragged laugh came from inside the bar.

Stu turned toward the door, but the biker with the patchy blond beard took his arm and turned him back around. "I used to work over there," he said, pointing with his fuzzy chin toward the nuke plant. He aimed the full force of his bad breath into Stu's face. "Used to make me go under the vessel."

"What?"

"Where the machinery's at. Under them domes. Hot every way there is to *be* hot—a whole barbecue of ways to die down in there."

A sort of chant was going on inside the bar, and there were more of those screams that might have been, but were not really, pleasure.

"Man had to stay cool," Patchy said, "badge on your wrist going red. Too many goddamn rads. You know?"

"Radical," said the biker with the long black hair.

"Radiation. You can't see it do what it does, but it still does it. Shit, crawling under the vessel. Fuck that. Had you wear a vest with ice in it so you could stand the heat. Ice vest to make you think you's cooler than you was."

A sob turned Stu around again, and he was at the door before he knew it. Bang stood up to block his way, but Stu could still see the Wiggler. She stood in the middle of a circle of chairs. Each guy held a small plastic bag in one hand, and the Wiggler went from guy to guy, braving their free hands and trying to grab a bag.

"What's she trying to get?" Stu asked.

Bang scoffed. "Little forty-dollar bag."

Always the bags receded before her grasp and the empty hands came. She squealed in their grasps like a badly played instrument.

One guy grabbed her hair and pulled the Wiggler's head back. Stu could see. Nobody was at home in those eyes. He turned away. There were memories for him in these waters. No feelings, he reminded himself, no fear. He pulled a twenty from his wallet and held out to Bang. "How about adding a case of Blue Crab to that?"

Bang did not hear. Bang did not see.

Stu drew out his last bill, a ten.

Bang wrapped the money in his fist and pulled it away. Then he leaned in close. "I'll sell you a case of our beer if you bring that bitch back here before Friday, and no Rickie."

Stu shrugged. What did he owe her? "I could try," he said.

"You walk outta here with our beer and you'll do better than try," Bang said. "That piece of shit crabbing boat of yours can't hide nowhere for long."

"Okay," Stu said. "But I'm not her daddy or nothing."

"Bitch ain't got a daddy," Bang said. Then he turned and disappeared into the bar.

Stu went back to the railing. The tide was going out, and mud showed around the edges of the anchorage, black and stinking. Across the bay loomed the nuke plant. Its cooling tower was narrow at the waist. The containment domes were like breasts.

This was bad. Memories lurked like snags—his wife as a young woman in the hands of other men, his daughter gone some place where the body wouldn't follow.

Patchy came onto the porch and set a case of beer by Stu's feet. Out in the channel a container ship went by, thrumming its diesel reggae.

The Wiggler came onto the porch after a while and put a hand in the middle of Stu's back. She was back in her eyes, more or less, and she waggled a little packet. "Got it," she said.

Stu picked up the beer, and they walked together down the steps.

"How'd you manage that?" the Wiggler said, nodding at the case.

Stu gave her the Eskimo smile.

They crossed the beach and walked out to the end of   the pier.

By the time Stu cranked the diesel and untied the lines, the Wiggler had finished her business at the chart table and sat in the mate's seat sniffling and smiling.

"Nothing's like speed," she said. "Nothing in the whole world. Makes you, you know, enough."

Stu motored past the breakwater. The wind had died down, and the tide was almost all the way out.

Soon, the Wiggler was back at the table, making more lines. At that rate, it wouldn't be long before she'd need another trip to the Bayview.

She snorted and then folded her arms, looking into the distance like somebody trying to make out a faint sound. Her hands dropped to her sides, and she looked at Stu. "This is shit," she said. "Ain't crystal." She wet her finger, dipped it into the bag, and then touched it to her tongue. "Shit." Her shoulders slumped and she sat in the mate's seat. "After all that, they gave me shit."

"Want to head back?"

"No," she said. "I need Rickie. Rickie scores for me."

"Couldn't hurt to try," Stu said.

The Wiggler looked at him. Her forehead wrinkled. "Is that what you think?"

"We could turn right around," Stu said. "I don't even mind."

"No," she said, "I gotta find Rickie."

Stu shrugged. "Suit yourself." Then he set a course to   his traps.

"Where you going?"

"Check my pots."

"But, the marina."

"This won't take long."

The Wiggler winced. "If you were in my skin, you'd think different about how long long is." She sat there with her chin in her hands. Slowly, her eyes glazed, and she stared vacantly forward.

When they got to his traps, he slowed and maneuvered to pick up the first buoy. He ran the line over the pulley and hit the switch. The boat leaned as the winch strained to lift the trap from the mud. It broke free finally, and the boat rocked. When the trap was clear of the water, Stu swung it aboard and opened the door. A dozen crabs poured out and clattered into the corners of the sorting table, claws raised.

"Ugh," said the Wiggler.

"What?"

"Big shit-eating spiders if you ask me." She kept rubbing her arms.

Stu stuck two bunkers in the trap for bait, closed the door, and dropped the pot back into the bay. He drew on his gloves then and started the sort. Little ones went back into the bay, and the keepers went into a basket.

"Why don't they just crawl out of the traps the same way they go in?" The Wiggler said.

He didn't know why. They just went for what they wanted, he supposed, and by the time they got it, it was too late. "Some do," he said. "Most don't."

"Stupid," the Wiggler said. She rubbed her temples with her fingertips.

"Yep." At the end of the count, Stu picked up a crab that held another crab in its arms.

"What's with them?"

"Soft-shell," Stu said. "They've got to shed to grow, and for a few days they're soft as you or me. That other one puts itself on top to protect it."

"Huh," the Wiggler said. "Crab love."

"It's just instinct. Soft ones bring good money," Stu said. "There may be more." He peeled the soft-shell out of the arms of its protector.

"Aw," said the Wiggler, "leave it alone."

"What?"

"Let it go."

"They're just crabs."

The Wiggler's eyes sparked. She seemed nervous and exhausted at the same time. "And maybe you're just a prick."

Stu put the soft-shell on ice in the cooler. He closed the lid and stood. The Wiggler was staring fire at him.

"They live a long time on ice," he said, but he didn't need to explain anything to her. It was none of her business. Turned out that he preferred her empty-eyed and absent. "Soft-shells bring twice what regular crabs do."

"I don't care," she said. "It ain't right."

Stu throttled up and headed for the next float. He grabbed the line with the boat hook, but as soon as he looped it over the pulley, the Wiggler took it off again. "Stop it," he said.

"No."

"Listen!" He wanted to call her out, wanted to put her in her place. What was she thinking, coming onto his boat and messing with his fishing? "Listen, Wiggler . . ."

"What'd you call me?"

"What everybody calls you."

"Well fuck you," she said. "And fuck them." She put her hands on the gunwale and looked down at the water. "My name's Karen. Got it?"

"Sure," Stu said, but he could not fit the name to the whore he had seen in the grip of those men.

"My name's Karen and I've got a one-year-old whose goddamned daddy whales on her and there's not a fucking thing I can do about it. You know what I'm saying?"

Whoa, Stu thought, but he didn't know what to say.

The next trap held even more soft-shells. Stu pried them loose and carried the shedders to the cooler. They couldn't even lift their claws they were so helpless.

The tide was so low that the winch pulled the next trap up in just seconds. Stu sorted through the catch and laid the soft-shells in the cooler.

The Wiggler glared, arms folded across her chest.

"What's wrong with you?" he said.

"You wanna know?"

He shook his head. "I suppose not," he said.

"I got to get out of this life," she said. "But there's nothing like meth. It makes you . . . enough, you know?"

"Until it's gone."

"I gotta get my kid," she said. "I need somebody."

"Wanna head back to the Bayview?" he said.

The Wiggler stared down at the cooler, her face slack.

That was better, Stu thought. That was safer, deeper water. His own memories were sunk down deep like that.

He was about to hook the next line when he heard a splash and looked back to see the cooler floating upside-down in the water behind the boat.

"I don't give a shit," the Wiggler said. "You shouldn't do it to start with, you son of a bitch." She reached for the basket with the regular crabs in it, but Stu blocked her and said, "Stop!" He pulled the basket close. Then he turned 247 around and came up alongside the cooler. It was empty.

"They'll just get eaten by everything down there, now," he told her, but she was staring at the water.

He set a course for the Basin. Tomorrow. He could check the rest of his traps tomorrow when he was alone the way he ought to be. All he wanted now was to get the Wiggler off his boat. She was a mess, and she spread messes wherever she went.

The tide was so low by the time they got back that 247 churned mud as it made its way through the mouth of the Basin. Stu threaded his way toward his slip, but the last run was all mud. It'd take half an hour for the tide to turn and another hour for the water to rise far enough for him to get into his slip.

The Wiggler had his binoculars. She was looking for Rickie or his boat or his bike. "Nothing," she said. "Where *is* he?"

All Stu wanted was to give Bo his case of beer and to add an Eskimo smile when Bo asked how he got it. He wanted to let thoughts of bikers and Wigglers sink back beneath the waves. He put 247 in reverse and backed up twenty feet. Then he threw it into forward and hit the throttle. The boat squatted, its propeller churning the bottom. The bow plowed into the mud, sending fiddler crabs down their holes. But 247 did not get far. Stu frowned and shut the motor down. "Gotta wait," he said.

"How long?"

"Hour, two."

"God," she said. "He's not here anywhere."

The mud stank. Everything that had ever died and rotted was in that stink, and there was nothing Stu could do except wait for the tide to come back and cover it all with clean salty water that could make you forget about things like bottoms.

He stood there behind the wheel, looking at his slip just forty feet away.

The Wiggler came up next to him and nudged her shoulder under his arm. "I've got to get out of this life," she said.

Stu could not remember the last time someone touched him. The Wiggler was so thin, too thin. Years ago, he had crashed his daughter's wedding and danced briefly with her. When he asked if she was happy, all she had done was shrug. Stu thought it was her way of saying it was none of his business. He shook his head, there on the boat, and tried not to think. No feelings, no fear. But it had been there all along, his daughter's real answer, just beneath the surface. She was in the hands of her mother and her stepfather and her bright, shiny husband, and she needed somebody.

"Thank you," the Wiggler said, "for trying to help."

Stu shook his head. "I didn't."

"But you tried."

Stu looked at her feet. They were filthy.

"I'm sorry I threw your crabs away."

He gave her the frozen smile. No feelings. But something welled up in him, and his throat tightened.

It made no sense.

He and Karen stood together on the slanted deck. 247 was mired in the stink. She snuggled against him. It was all wrong. What Stu needed was his daughter, his past. But there was no way back, he knew. There was nothing now, but time and the tides.

How Love Feels

Hope made you lean forward. It was humiliating, really, and Stu hated that his daughter could see him straining like that, wanting something so badly. But each time their rowboat came to a bend in the river, he could not restrain himself but had to twist around to look for a house, a bridge—some way to get to a phone. The woods slid aside like a slow curtain, but each reveal showed only more trees, more muddy banks, and another fetch of river as empty and disappointing as the last. He would sit there then, with the oars in his hands, and gaze back up the river.

The motor had run fine until mid-morning. Then, no matter how hard he pulled the start cord, the thing just spit and quit. Stu considered rowing to shore and walking back to his ex-wife's house. But sunlight filtered through the trees, all green and soothing, and it felt so good drifting down the river under that canopy that he decided to keep going while he worked on the motor. The banks were thick with green briars and broken by streams that cut muddy ravines. It would have been pure misery walking through such a mess as that anyway. And so they drifted.

Gloria rolled her eyes when he took the cover off the outboard. It was harder and harder for Stu to find things the two of them could enjoy when he came for his monthly visitations. This time he brought his little outboard motor from home so he and his seventeen-year-old daughter could use his ex-wife's boat to spend the day fishing.

Gloria had not liked the idea from the start. She did not fish anymore, she informed him. She had not fished since she was ten. She squinted at him, and her dark eyes roiled with resentments that Stu could not see the shape of.

He had driven halfway across the state to spend the day with her. What else were they to do? He had enough money for the trip back home but little more. He had it in his mind that she might like to fish.

She stared balefully at him, but she went.

With his pocketknife and a pair of pliers, he broke the carburetor down, blew out the jets and ports as best he could, and then put it together again. But after an hour, the motor still refused to start. It was embarrassing. He had been a waterman for twenty years, and he had a knack for mechanical things. A dozen times, he had gotten himself back to land by fixing engine problems. He was proud of this, and he had wanted to take his daughter fishing so that she could see him in his element.

"I think it's the gas," he said. "It must be old gas in the tank."

Gloria said nothing. Everything made her unhappy. Ever since the abortion six months earlier, she had wanted nothing to do with Stu. Still, he leaned forward in his heart, hoping that around each bend in the conversation he might find her, waiting for him, smiling, glad to see him, glad he was still in her life.

By the time he gave up on the motor, they had drifted so far from his ex-wife's house that there was no choice but to keep going. Eventually they'd come to a bridge where they could get a ride to a phone someplace. So they swung through bend after bend, from hope to disappointment and back again until Venus rose into the indigo sky, and Stu had to put hope away for the night. He leaned back in his seat, steadied his voice, and told his daughter that they'd have to stop.

She slitted her eyes and punched buttons on her phone even though it had died two hours into the trip.

An old gum tree leaned out, nearly horizontal, from the bank, and as they drifted by Stu grabbed a branch. The boat swung around behind the tree and settled in next to a steep and muddy bank six feet high.

Gloria sat there in the bow and looked at her father. "I have a date tonight, you know."

"Oh?"

"Can we walk from here?"

"Honey, it'll be dark soon, and we don't even have a flashlight."

"Well, why don't we? Jesus. You mean we stay *here*?"

It was Stu's turn to pause.

Gloria pulled herself up onto the tree's trunk. Stu handed her the gallon jug of water and what was left of their lunches. He tied the boat to a limb and pulled the stringer from the water. A smallmouth bass and a good-sized catfish dangled from the line. He climbed up next to Gloria, and they both inched carefully along the tree until they came to the roots, which made a knuckly sort of ladder to dry land.

Stu made a small fire, and then he knelt by the fish. Gloria folded her arms and turned away when he split the bass open and scooped out its guts.

Stu stuck the fish on green sticks and roasted them like hot dogs, and when the meat began to smell like food, Gloria turned back toward the fire and took one of the sticks. There was some salt in Stu's lunch bag, and the fish was wonderful.

Even Gloria dissolved into "ahs" and "ums."

When there was nothing left but bones, Stu asked her what she thought her mother and stepfather would be doing back at her house now.

Gloria closed her eyes. "Probably," she said, and her eyes opened as if she had glimpsed a vision, "Steppie the Dad is pissed." Gloria pulled a sapling out of the ground. "Ken's the boss," she said. "Ken runs the show. He's on the phone, making and shaking."

"Worried."

"Pissed," she said, and she walked the sapling on its roots and fluttered the leaves like arms. "Gloria's gone and done something without permission again!"

When the fire died down and the woods began to get dark, Stu spread a tarp on the ground for Gloria. She pulled half of it over herself for a blanket. Stu made himself a bed of leaves by the fire. The mosquitoes were bad, but he dosed himself with repellent before lying down.

"And this date?" Stu said.

The river current muttered in the roots of the trees.

"Works for Steppie." Gloria seemed bored by the subject. "Hand-picked, pedigreed breeder just for me." She raised herself on one elbow. "Supervisor in the Tree Room."

Ken ran a specialty nursery business, sending rare plants to buyers around the country. He was just what Stu's ex-wife had always wanted in a husband—powerful, rich.

The fire was only a glow now, but Stu saw a frown pass over Gloria's face.

"They dig up these little trees," she said, "and they wash all the dirt off their roots, and stick their tops in this machine that beats the leaves off. Then they stack them on their sides in this, like, dungeon where it's cold and dark and damp. They don't die, though. Even though they got pulled up, they don't die." Her eyes were pooling. Stu could see them glistening in the fire glow. "But they don't grow, either. They're just there with their ugly roots sticking out, waiting. Maybe they get mailed out, and maybe not. Maybe they just get thrown away because they can't stay in the dungeon forever, you know."

Stu wanted to ask her if this was the boy who had gotten her pregnant. But what he asked instead was, "How old is he?"

He must have stiffened when she said twenty-eight because Gloria snorted a laugh. "I need somebody with a future. Mom says you can never tell with boys my age."

"So who's dating this guy, you or your mother?"

Gloria lay back down and stretched out. "She was too young to know how to pick a man when . . . when she married you. That's what she says."

"What do you say?"

Gloria shrugged.

The embers winked out, one by one, until only glowworms and fireflies showed in the dark woods.

"I used to listen to my mother," Stu said. "She told me I could heal people with my touch. I was just a little thing, but she said I was a seventh son and so God had chosen me."

Gloria was up on her elbow again. "Seventh?"

Stu wanted to kick himself. He was just trying to help, but this could not wind up in a good place. Why was he forever drifting toward disaster? "Seven by her count."

"But—"

"Vernon got killed in Vietnam, Kenny in a car wreck."

"That's only three, counting you."

What could he do? Time just seemed to drag him over the falls every time. "Your grandmother," he said. "She counted everybody."

Gloria was silent.

The embers ticked, cooling.

"It doesn't end," Gloria said. "It's like somebody's knocking on a door that I just can't open now."

"What I was trying to say is maybe it's not always best to listen to your mom."

Gloria lay back down, and Stu felt her turn away. "So," she said, "you're a healer."

*   *   *

The morning dawned gray, and the woods along the river dripped with dew. Stu picked leaves out of his hair and washed his face and hands in the river. For breakfast, they shared some crackers from Gloria's lunch bag, and there was still plenty of water in the jug. They packed up, then, and without a word got back in the boat.

The mist burned away by mid-morning. Then, just after noon, they rounded a turn and saw a high bridge. Stu's heart soared. They tied up and watched the swallows swoop in the bridge's shadow. It was a railroad bridge, but still, Stu thought there might be houses nearby. A quarter mile walk through thick brush and then a steep climb up the bluff got them to the grade, where the tracks disappeared into the distance with nothing but woods on either side. They walked along for half a mile anyway, hoping that they might find a house. But all they found were scuppernong grapes hanging from vines that choked the trees. The smell was overpowering—sweet and fermented.

Gloria picked a grape and pinched it. The thick skin split, and the meat oozed out. She sucked it into her mouth and then spat out the seeds. "I have a date tonight, too," she said. "And this is turning out to be really stupid."

"He's going to think you're calling it off if we don't get back soon—stood up two nights in a row."

Gloria led the way back to the boat, and they shoved off. All afternoon, the river grew. Trees parted above them, and the sky shone a deep blue. Hope wound and unwound, but there was not a road or a house to be seen. Then, in mid-afternoon, they rounded a bend and there, through the tangle of trees and vines, Stu saw lines that seemed unnaturally straight. He slowed, rowing gently against the current. As they got closer, the lines emerged and connected, and it was a house. Stu pulled the boat onto the little beach out front. The trees were tall, and the shade was deep. There was a bird's nest under the eaves at the door to the front porch. Stu knocked, even though he already knew no one was there. The place smelled of mildew and rotting wood. He peered in the windows. Old mismatched furniture, cots, a camp stove. There were no phone wires, no power lines, not even a road leading in. It was just a fishing shack, something to keep off the rain and mosquitoes. The door was unlocked, and Stu went in hoping to find some canned food, but there was nothing.

If he didn't get them to a phone soon, they were going to spend another night in the woods, and Stu would miss work on Monday. He didn't even want to think about what his ex-wife was going to do. How could he have turned a simple afternoon with his daughter into such a disaster? His brain seemed to squirm in his skull. He walked back onto the porch, where Gloria was curled up in a hammock with her eyes closed.

"Nothing," he said as calmly as he could manage.

She opened her eyes. "Gee Sus Christ."

"I'm sorry, honey. Your tree guy's going to be upset."

"No," she said, "it's Ryan—different guy."

"Oh."

They got in the boat, and Stu shoved them off. Late in the afternoon, they came upon an old bridge piling, the last remnant of a road that must have disappeared in the fifties. The concrete was crumbling, and reinforcing rods stuck out the top, all twisted and rusty. Drift logs had piled up at the base, and the water pouring through made a rushing sound. Gloria looped a line over a log, and the boat swung around behind the piling and settled into the dead water. Stu baited a hook and quickly caught a couple of knotty heads. They were bony, trash fish, but he was hungry and so he put them on the stringer anyway. A half hour passed without a bite. The sun beat down on them, and flies orbited their heads.

"So," said Gloria, "you do this for a living, huh?"

Stu was ready to go, but when Gloria reeled in, she found a catfish that had swallowed the bait and then just stayed, calmly, in place. "I don't get it," she said.

Stu dug into the cat's throat with pliers and grimaced as he tried to work the hook out gently. The cat made croaking sounds. Stu did his best, but finally he shut his eyes and tore the hook from the cat's throat. He threaded the stringer through its gills and dropped the fish overboard.

Gloria leaned over and watched it. "Ryan's a picker," she said. "Works in the fields. Not good enough," she said. "Not for me. Want to know what he said? Said he didn't care whose kid it was, he'd marry me anyway and take care of us both. You believe that?"

"He must love you."

"Like a dog."

"So why date him then?"

Gloria peered into the water. "It feels good to be loved."

Stu untied the boat and moved them into the current. The sun beat down through the gap between the trees. He moved the boat back into the shade, but there, near the bank, the current almost disappeared.

"Doesn't the Tree Room guy love you?"

"Sure," she shrugged. "He's got plans."

The river slowed, and Stu started rowing steadily. After a while, the current disappeared altogether, and the water took on an oily stillness. If he stopped rowing, the boat stopped. It didn't take long for his back to begin aching.

The bends came and went more slowly now. Trees pulled back from the water, and reeds and cattails lined the shore. Red-winged blackbirds and herons replaced the woodpeckers and wood ducks they had been seeing. It was hot, and he was tired. With his back turned toward the front of the boat, he could not see the bends coming as easily and so it was harder to hope.

Then in the distance, they heard the buzz of an outboard motor.

"It's the reservoir," Gloria said.

"Finally," Stu said. "Would you pull the stringer in?"

She laid the fish in the bottom of the boat. The knotty heads were dead but the catfish was still breathing. Gloria stared at them. "It wasn't Ryan's," she said. "It was Mister Tree Room Supervisor's. He wasn't ready."

The wind was against them now. If Stu stopped rowing, they drifted backwards. Near twilight, they rounded the final bend and saw the distant lights from the marina at the head of the reservoir. The wind freshened, and after an hour's rowing, they had gone almost nowhere. Stu was exhausted. "We're going to have to stop," he said.

They set up camp on a sandy bank. Stu asked Gloria to clean the fish. She narrowed her eyes, but she knelt by the stringer and slit open a knotty and scooped out its guts. When she cut the head off, her teeth were clenched, and if it hadn't been for the tears, she would have looked vicious. Slowly, the anger left her face, and she cleaned the rest with a distant look. She didn't even flinch when she cleaned the fish that was still alive.

"He said I needed to grow up," she said. "Be a woman."

Stu cooked the fish, but there was no salt and the knotty heads were bland. They ate, but it was merely refueling. After dinner, Gloria collected pine boughs and made a mat she could lay the tarp on. They sat by the fire and watched the stars come out. Lights from the marina stretched long fingers over the water. Gloria tried to turn her phone on for the seven thousandth time, but she put it away after just one try. "I need a shower," she said, "and to wash my hair, and I want a real meal." She pulled saplings from the sandy soil and fed them to the fire.

"Take my advice," Stu said. "Go for the guy who loves you."

"But you're not . . ." Gloria could not seem to find words for what she was trying to say. "I mean, you don't . . ."

Stu knew. He was not successful. He lived in a trailer and fished for a living. What use was advice from somebody like him?

"You'll be eighteen soon," Stu said. "You can do what you want."

"I don't know what I want."

Stu's mother used to say that when you didn't know what to do, you shouldn't do a thing. But he wondered now if it had been good advice, if it had helped him in his life.

"What's wrong with the picker boy other than that he's poor?"

"You don't understand."

A distant outboard buzzed, and there were faint sounds of, perhaps, music blowing across the lake.

"She pushes and pushes and never drops the subject," Gloria said. "And then there's Steppie with his 'incentives' and his 'strategic positioning for the future.'"

"Your mother was pregnant when I married her."

"I know."

She knew because Stu had told her. He had also told her that the pregnancy ended in a miscarriage just three weeks after the wedding. But he had not told Gloria the rest: "The kid wasn't mine," he said.

Gloria pulled a sapling from the fire and extinguished it in the sand.

"I loved her," Stu said. "I would have loved her forever if she had been able to love me back."

Gloria nodded, but she wouldn't look at him. "It feels good to be loved," she said.

"Supposed to."

*   *   *

The sun was shining full on them when Stu woke up. He had slept surprisingly well. The yellow morning light shined like butter in the dew. Gloria woke up a little later, circles under her eyes, and when Stu asked how she had slept, she shrugged and said nothing. They packed the boat and got back on the water. By mid-morning, the breeze had freshened, and for once it blew in the right direction so that Stu didn't have to row much to make steady progress. It was not even noon when they could make out the sign at the gas dock, and by 12:30, they were tied up there.

Stu bought sticky buns and coffee and got change for the phone. Gloria fished from the dock while Stu made the call.

"They're coming," he told her. "Bringing my truck and your mom's car with the boat trailer. She's pissed. Kept calling it kidnapping. Told me to tell you goodbye and that she'd see me in court."

Gloria jerked her rod upward and began to reel in. The tip pointed at the water and shivered. When the fish was just below the dock, Gloria stopped reeling. She reached into the tackle box, pulled out a knife, and cut the line. The rod bobbed upward, and the cut end of the line fell back through the eyes of the rod.

"You're old enough to make your own decisions, you know."

Calmly, she took another hook from the tackle box and re-rigged. Then she skewered a fresh worm on the hook. It writhed as the barb pierced its body

"We have to try to explain," Stu said. "It was a mistake. The gas was old. We're sorry."

Gloria rolled her eyes.

When his truck drove into the boatyard with Ken at the wheel, Stu had the strange sensation that someone else had inherited his life. His ex came a moment later, driving her car with the boat trailer behind it. The highways had taken them farther in two hours than the river took Stu and Gloria in two days.

JoAnna got out of the car and walked across the parking lot toward Stu and Gloria. She was still slim and lovely with dark, bottomless eyes. Her face, though, was stony.

"Are you okay?" she asked Gloria.

Gloria shrugged.

"Get in the car," she said. "I'll be there in a minute."

"JoAnna," Stu said, "we need to explain. Gloria . . ." He reached out to put an arm around her, but Gloria was already walking toward the car.

"We thought we'd find a phone sooner," Stu said. "It was a mistake. I'm sorry."

JoAnna would not look at him.

Ken backed the trailer down the ramp and into the water while Gloria sat in the back seat staring forward like someone who had been picked up by the cops.

"Actually," JoAnna said, "I'm grateful to you, Stu. You are living proof of what I've been telling her all along."

"Don't make her marry that guy, JoAnna. He doesn't love her. We should talk about this."

JoAnna backed up a step, and Stu realized that he had been leaning forward, looming over her. "You want her to marry the other one?" JoAnna said. Her eyes deepened for a moment. "The one who never manages to actually do anything? I'm not worried about that," she said. "She won't marry that kid." She squinted the way Gloria did. "You know why?"

Stu watched Ken load the boat and pull it up the ramp. It sat there dripping water onto the parking lot.

"You," JoAnna said. "You are the reason she will not marry that kid, and, like I told you, Stu, I'm grateful." Then she was gone, across the parking lot and into the car.

Stu watched them leave. Gloria blew him a kiss from the back seat, and then they were gone. He crossed the lot toward his truck. A pay phone hung forlornly from a telephone pole, its ravaged phone book curling in the sun. He should do something, call someone. He stood there fingering the handset and staring out at the boatyard. The travel lift, with its I-beams and its winches and its huge straps for carrying boats, was parked in the midst of rotting hulks. The straps hung down, empty. There was no one to call. Stu got into his truck and stared through the windshield at the shore of the reservoir. It stretched out in a long line, without a single bend or cove, not a bay or a nook in sight, no place at all where hope might be hiding.

JoAnna's
Story

She was driving far too fast, but she needed to get home. It was late, and she had said an awful thing at the party. Now she just wanted to crawl into bed and sleep, if she could. "I'm so glad the bitch is gone," JoAnna had said of her sister, Campbell. It was supposed to be a joke—one of those bad, sad, healing kinds of jokes. But her friend Stacy had nodded and frowned. It was awful. The expression on Stacy's face had revealed JoAnna to herself—she, the younger sister, the not-so-pretty one, the not-so-talented one, was actually glad that her sister was dead.

Now, all she wanted was to snuggle into the bed that had been hers since she was a little girl—a little girl who idolized her big sister. She kept her foot on the gas as she entered the big curve. The Buick's tires slid sideways on the gravel and it took only a moment for the car to get sideways. When the wheels hit the embankment, the Buick rose into the air. The engine revved, and JoAnna got her foot off the gas and onto the brake as if she might be able to stop what had already been set in motion. But the car nosed downward, and JoAnna's stomach rose into her throat. The impact was softer than she expected. Mud splattered the windshield, and the headlights must have been buried in it, because by the time the car settled, everything was darkness except for the dash. JoAnna sat there blinking stupidly. One red light said "Oil." The other, "Charge."

It took a moment before she realized that water would soon begin pouring in, and who knew where it would stop? She unhooked her seatbelt and pulled the door handle, but the door would not budge.

She put her feet against it and pushed, but that just made her slide across the seat. She lay down and braced her hands against the other door. Then she pushed with everything she had, but it was as if she wasn't even there. She panicked. She pounded the window until her hands throbbed. "Goddamn," she sobbed, and that was when it occurred to her to roll the window down.

She slid out of the car feet first and dropped into the muck. Her legs disappeared to the knees, and bubbles formed inside her jeans and wriggled their way up. As soon as she tried to take a step she was falling. Her hands sank into the mud and she wound up lying on her left side, face pillowed on the slimy cold. She crawled, and the mud pulled off both of her shoes. But she kept going until she got to the road, where she stood on the side and looked down at her parents' best car.

They were going to be furious. They had let her use it and had even extended her curfew to two o'clock so she could go to the game and then to the party at her friend's house afterwards. But JoAnna got drunk. She said that awful thing, and then she fell asleep. It was almost four when she woke up, and all she wanted was to get home. But now this.

She shook mud from her hands and set out walking down the gravel toward home. She came to the lonely intersection where Campbell had died. JoAnna shivered. Her bare feet were freezing.

It had happened in March—after the first big rain. The road was soupy, and the ditches were full. Her sister must have lost it in the curve, and the car careened into a culvert that ran under the intersection, plowing so far in that it disappeared from view.

Her parents were angry when Campbell was not home on time. They were sure she was running around with that spoiled kid. Her, their best girl—star hitter on the volleyball team, tall, beautiful, dark. Campbell, the model, the athlete, the honor student. It was just that boy who was the problem.

But the boy showed up the next day looking for Campbell, and then everything became awful.

They searched. They called. They put up posters, but there was no sign of Campbell.

The weather turned dry and cold, and a week later, after the ditches had begun to dry down, Mr. Gabriel was mowing with the Bush Hog when he peered into the culvert and caught a glint of glass.

The crushed dashboard had pinned Campbell's legs. The police would not say more than that. And all the questions JoAnna and her parents had were too horrible to ask.

JoAnna's mother drifted like a ghost through the days that led to the funeral. After the guests were gone and the family had to start again, the emptiness in her mother filled with fury. JoAnna could do nothing right, could be nothing right. And JoAnna's father had no idea how to help anyone because there was nothing for his hands to do. He would look at them sometimes, as if they belonged to someone else.

JoAnna's feet grew numb as she walked. She tried to push hair from her face, but it was caked with mud. She could only imagine what she must look like, and then she realized that there was no way she could show up at home like that.

The security light at the Garbiels' place shone in the distance. JoAnna turned into their lane and walked the quarter mile to their house. A light was on in the kitchen and she didn't have to knock long before Mrs. Gabriel's round face appeared at the door. Her eyes went wide, though, and she lurched backward into her living room, her hands at her mouth.

JoAnna sank to the porch floor, shivering.

In a moment, the storm door creaked and Mrs. Gabriel's hand was on her shoulder. "I didn't realize. Jo? Honey? It's you. Yes? My lord child. What happened?"

"I ran into the ditch."

"God!" Mrs. Gabriel pulled her hand away as if it burned. "Are you hurt?"

JoAnna shrugged.

Mrs. Gabriel helped her to her feet and took her inside. She sat her at the kitchen table and put a towel over her shoulders like a shawl. "I'll call your folks," she said and picked up the phone. But she did not dial. She stared at JoAnna. "No," she said. She replaced the handset. "We've got to clean you up first. Are you okay? No broken bones? No cuts?"

"I'm cold."

Mrs. Gabriel helped her stand and took her upstairs to the bathroom. She turned on the shower and got JoAnna out of her muddy clothes. The water felt wonderful. JoAnna stood under it, watching black water flow down the drain. She washed her hair, and got a surprising amount of mud out of her left ear. After a while, the shivering stopped. She was drying off when Mrs. Gabriel tapped the door and told her that she had put some clean clothes there for her. JoAnna wrapped herself in the towel and opened the door.

The clothes were on the floor—sweatpants and a sweatshirt. They must have belonged to Becky, the Gabriels' only child, who was married now and living up North. It felt strange not having underwear on, but somehow warm and cozy, too, like pajamas.

On her way downstairs to the kitchen, JoAnna could hear Mrs. Gabriel telling her husband, Sandy, to get the tractor and pull the car out of that ditch. She did *not* want JoAnna's parents to see it there.

Mrs. Gabriel had made coffee and was sitting at the table with a mug. She smiled when JoAnna came into the kitchen. "I haven't seen that sweatshirt on anybody for years. Cup?"

"Yes, please," JoAnna said. She sat at the table. "Thank you. For everything."

"It's okay, honey. At least you're not hurt. Everything else can be fixed. Sandy's getting your car out. He'll bring it back, and we'll see what it needs."

"I feel so stupid."

"It's a bad road." Mrs. Gabriel got up and poured a cup. "Sugar?"

"Yes. But I know it's bad," JoAnna said. "I should know better than just about anybody how bad it is."

Mrs. Gabriel sat down and slid the cup and sugar forward. She sipped coffee and gazed over her mug at JoAnna. "You look so much like her. It must be a comfort for your mom."

When you took each piece by itself, she did look like Campbell—the nose, the chin, the eyes—they were Campbell's but put together in a different way, a not-so-beautiful way, a long-faced way. Her mother often slipped and called her by her sister's name these days.

She would frown though, and shake her head. And JoAnna could hear disappointment in her voice when she corrected herself.

"I saw something about you in the paper," Mrs. Gabriel said. "What was it volleyball, college?

No, that would have been Campbell. JoAnna played piccolo in the band. "I was on the B honor roll last term," she said.

"Ah." Mrs. Gabriel sipped coffee. "That must have been it." She gazed at the window.

JoAnna had never failed anything, had never even gotten a C. But when it came to being as good as Campbell, her grade was always "needs improvement." Boys from rich families never stood in line for a chance to date JoAnna. They never picked her up in their expensive cars, never took her to fancy restaurants. No, the closest JoAnna had ever come to being like her big sister was tonight when she had risen out of the ditch like a ghost.

Mrs. Gabriel drained the last of her coffee. The faintest hint of gray showed in the eastern sky. "Well," she said. "I'll call now. At least there's a little light."

She should have made the call herself, JoAnna knew, but she could not face it.

Mrs. Gabriel had barely finished dialing when she said, "Well, you must have been right by the phone. This is Grace. Yes." Mrs. Gabriel's face was patience. "Yes," she said. "Here. Yes. Here. She's fine. Just a little mishap with the car. No. She's fine. Wait. She needs shoes. Hello? Yes. Shoes. Good . . ." Mrs. Gabriel hung up. She looked at JoAnna. "They're coming."

JoAnna was going to get it now. She had wrecked the car. She had not called right away, and her parents had worried for what must have seemed like forever. Why hadn't she called? Why didn't she think about how they would have worried when she didn't make it home on time, or when she wasn't there when they got up, if they had been able to sleep at all, that is? God, she was stupid. At least when Campbell didn't come home she had a good reason, the best reason.

The Impala came racing up the Gabriels' lane, and in no time, her mother was at the back door. She was dressed and her hair was dry, so JoAnna knew that she must have been up all night.

"Where is she?" she said before Mrs. Gabriel could even open the door.

JoAnna stood up. "I'm here," she said.

There was no hello to Mrs. Gabriel. No thank you for calling. There was just fury. JoAnna thought she understood. Her mother was furious at Campbell for dying, furious because Campbell was not there for her to be furious at, furious because others had lived, others who maybe had less of a right to it than Campbell did.

Her mother stepped around Mrs. Gabriel and into the room. She frowned and looked at JoAnna as if she could not place her. Her forehead wrinkled. "What are you wearing?"

"They're Becky's," Mrs. Gabriel said. "Her clothes got muddy."

"Muddy? How?"

JoAnna and Mrs. Gabriel looked at each other. No one wanted to start the story.

JoAnna's father drove up in his truck and stopped next to the Impala. He got out and looked back up the drive. There was Mr. Gabriel's tractor groaning up the lane pulling the Buick. Its tires flung chunks of mud from the wheel wells, and the front end was packed with cattails.

JoAnna's mother turned toward her. She was more furious than ever. "What happened?"

"Lost it in the curve," JoAnna said. "Hit the ditch."

Kids did that all the time in the county. The ditches were wide and gently sloped. Fences were set well off the road. It seemed sometimes that the ditches were like safety nets, and kids tried impossible things on the dirt roads because they thought there was nothing to worry about.

"But you," her mother said, "are okay?"

It sounded like an accusation. The one kid in the county who ought to have known better didn't. She had done a stupid thing, but she was fine. The best died, her mother was probably thinking, but you couldn't kill the worst with a sledgehammer. Her mother stood in front of her, squinting as if she was trying to bring her into focus. "*Are* you okay?" Her smile was like a wince.

No. She was not okay. She wanted to die. She wanted to get rid of the long-faced imitation that did nothing but make her mother miserable.

"JoAnna," her mother said. "Are you okay?"

A million times she had answered that question with a shrug and a "sure." What else could she do? You couldn't fix failure, stupid, or ugly by admitting to them.

JoAnna shrugged. "Sure," she said, but the tears had started, and they would not stop.

Her mother's eyes glazed over, and she held out her arms and pulled JoAnna to her. She squeezed and squeezed. She leaned back and cradled JoAnna's face in her hands. "We were so worried," she said. "I couldn't stand it." Her eyes were full. She hugged JoAnna and rocked her back and forth. "JoAnna," she said. "JoAnna, JoAnna."

And that name, that plain-Jane name, rang in JoAnna's ears like a bell.

Her father was standing there all of a sudden holding a pair of women's fur-lined boots in his hand, pleasure and pain at war on his face. He put a hand on JoAnna's head. "Child . . ." he said. Then he lifted the hand and set the boots on the floor. He went back outside. JoAnna could see him over her mother's shoulder talking to Mr. Gabriel. The two of them walked around the car surveying the mess. Her parents had sold Campbell's car for salvage so they would never have to see it again. But her father would fix this car. He would take the ditch out of it and make it seem as if the accident had never happened. And he would be happy because there would be something useful for his hands.

Her mother leaned back and held JoAnna at arm's length. "Sit," she said.

JoAnna sat in the kitchen chair, and her mother knelt on the floor in front of her. One at a time, she slipped the fur-lined boots onto JoAnna's bare feet. Then she looked up, eyes glistening. They felt wonderful, those boots and those eyes, and JoAnna wondered if this was what it was like to be the most beautiful, the favorite daughter.

Stu's Story

He was feverish and weak and drifting in a rowboat with no oars, but Stuart was not afraid. In low places along the shore, willow trees leaned out, hanging their hair over the water. It was low tide, and breezes that smelled like dead fish pushed him toward the shore where the roofs of people's houses barely showed above the foxtail reeds.

They shot and stabbed, Stu had heard. Washing machines and old cars rusted in their little yards, and fallen trees lay like skeletons in the mud of the swamp behind their houses.

No, Stu was not afraid. He would come back from this. Rivers moved like the in and out of breath. For half an hour at dead low tide, it was like the world had been punched in the stomach. It hunched there unable to breathe, unable to do what it had to do. But if you waited, the air would go salty and the tide would pour back in, urgent with current and strong as before, but this time flowing the other way to cover the stink of low tide with clean salt water.

This morning, his father had threatened to kennel him with the coon dogs if he tried to sneak outside again.

Stu's mother had looked out the window. "He wants air," she said, "sunshine." She lifted her chin. "I guess he oughta know."

"He's a boy, Edna."

"With a grip on God," his mother pointed out.

"He's a sick kid," his father said.

Stu was the seventh, and that was why sick people brought their troubles to his door. If he had not eaten yet that day, he could go out onto the back porch and stand, as only he could, on the pivot between well and sick. For a dollar, he would touch their troubles, and they would heal.

It was amazing. His mother had said so.

All morning long, Stu would touch, and the Mason jar she put on the steps grew greener.

But when Stu got sick, his parents fought. His father wanted a doctor. But his mother thought Stu should face God alone. The doctor finally got there, but he couldn't even find Stu. He shined a light in Stu's eyes and looked. He knocked on Stu's back and then listened, but Stu was gone—far down inside himself where fever and fatigue had made a place.

"Pneumonia," the doctor said.

"I told her," his father said.

When the doctor left, Stu's father leaned over and told him he had to rest. He couldn't go outside. "I don't care what your mother says. You hear me, son? Stu?"

But then his father left to get medicine, and Stu rose from his bed. He drifted downstairs, dizzy and weak as a ghost. Often he hunched over and coughed, gasping and racking through the minutes it took to work the sickness from of his chest. He held fistfuls of his shirt against the pain, and waited for his next breath.

Dizzy, he pulled open the back door and saw his mother in a chair under the oak where she argued with God. Kenny and Vernon, his two live brothers, sat next to each other on a low limb.

Stu ghosted past them to the shed. He picked up the rope and pulled, not with his arms, because his arms were like rubber; he just held on and leaned.

"Go back inside," said Kenny, the oldest. "Go back and be a sick little girlie."

"Sick don't make him better," said Vernon.

His mother's voice came from under the tree. She was half hidden by the leaves hanging down. "He's tired from wrestling God," she said. "Leave him be."

Kenny went back into the house, but Vernon helped Stu drag the boat to the river. Vernon hated him the most. He was sixth, and in the spring, he had to dig and hoe like everybody else while Stu only held the seeds and dropped them into the holes.

"He is the seventh," his mother explained. "His is the touch."

Vernon steadied the boat while Stu got in.

"Dad's going to get you good," he said. "All hell's going to break loose when he finds out what she let you do."

Stu slumped into the stern. In his fever, Vernon's voice hardly had any sound. The sun flashed on the water. He felt its warmth in his chest.

Vernon pushed the boat off the bank. The rocking felt good, and the boat turned lazily in the bright eddies.

"I pity you," Vernon said. "You notice something, Mister Big Shot?"

The boat corkscrewed slowly away.

"Notice you ain't got oars?"

His mother came out from under the tree, wiping wisps of hair from her face. "Not without oars," she said. "You get back here, Stu."

But the current had him by then.

"He don't need no oars," Vernon said. "He's such a big shot, he don't need a little thing like oars."

His mother swatted Vernon as if there was a fly on his head. "Get back here," she said to Stu.

"Tide's headed out," Vernon said. He held his hand up to fend off his mother's blows. "He'll wind up in Pressy's swamp."

His mother swatted at him as if his head was full of flies.

Vernon swung back at her this time, but her hand was at her mouth, and she watched Stu.

"Dad's going to get you for this," Vernon said. He was crying-mad.

His mother looked down at him and raised her hand.

"And Pressy's going to get him." Vernon pointed at Stu. "Going to cut him up for bait, like he did that dog."

The hand came down on Vernon's head, and Stu drifted around the bend.

Now, the dead-fish breeze pushed Stu toward a weeping willow tree that leaned out over the water.

His mother told him that people got rid of their troubles by digging holes under willow trees and crying their sorrows into them. They covered up the holes, and the trees did the crying after that.

Willow fronds hung like a curtain before him. He swept his hands through the water trying to back away, but the effort stirred up his sickness, and he bent over, racking and gasping and clutching his shirt. When he opened his eyes again, he had passed through the fronds and into the muddy gloom under the tree where cicadas wound and unwound their rattlesnake sounds, the rhythms all shifting and strange.

It took a while for his eyes to adjust, but slowly, he saw the catfish traps, gas cans, buckets, the parts of old outboard motors, the metal drums, plastic bottles, and right there by the waterside, a wheelbarrow beneath a cloud of flies.

The smell of death reached into Stu and tried to pull him inside out. He grabbed a handful of the willow's hair.

"You stealing," said a voice.

His mother had told him to be careful under willows not to dig up somebody else's troubles.

Stu pulled, but the fronds came loose and fell into the water.

A man stepped forward, then, a shadow coming from shadows—scraggly beard, deep wrinkles in his forehead. In one hand, he held a long, barked stick, tall as he was, and in the other a hammer. It was Pressy.

"Stealing my traps."

"No."

The man stared, but Stu was hiding down in his bed of sickness.

Pressy leaned his stick and his hammer against the tree. He reached into a bucket and drew out a catfish. He bent down and peered at Stu. Then he shook the catfish at him. "Look," he said, and he pressed the fish's belly against the trunk of the willow. He pulled a big nail from his pocket and pointed it at the back of the catfish's head. He looked over his shoulder at Stu. A handkerchief hung from the back of his hat to keep flies off his neck. "Ever been stabbed?" he said.

He picked up the hammer and tapped the nail. The fish quivered and curled its tail.

Stu tried to think what it was he wanted. Why he was there.

The man hammered the nail through the fish's head and into the trunk of the tree. The body went slack, but the gills kept moving in and out like wings.

One time, with his slingshot, Stu hit a sparrow in the head with a rock.

"Lucky shot," Vernon had said.

The bird fluttered under the oak and tipped. Stu ran to it and knelt. He folded it in his hands. It was warm and light, and its heart whirred in his palm. But then the beating stopped as if a wheel that had been spinning too fast just flew apart. The eyes went empty, and the bird slumped. Stu had always thought something flew away when you died, but the bird's heart just stopped and the body slumped.

"What's the matter, Mister Healer," Vernon had said, "killed it, didn't ya?"

Pressy put down the hammer. "Personally," he said, "I think they like it."

He took pliers from his back pocket and pulled the skin off the fish, like peeling a sock off a foot. It left the body white. "Oh yeah," he said. He flipped the skin into the wheelbarrow, and flies buzzed up into a storm. "They like it."

Stu doubled over and grabbed his shirt. What he worked from his lungs tasted like the smell under the willow. He spat into the water. "God," he said.

Flies settled back onto the wheelbarrow like a blue-black rain.

Pressy pointed his knife at Stu. "How come you got no oars? Huh? What you doing out here?"

Stu said nothing. He was just a little spark deep down in a world of darkness.

The man cut the fish's body from its head and pulled the insides out. He dipped the meat into a bucket of water and lifted it out again, shiny and white. Then he came down to the water's edge, his shoes crunching the empty husks of old cicadas. "You know what them boys that steal from me say first time they get stabbed?"

Stu was waiting for the tide, for the world to catch its breath and carry him back the way he came.

"You don't know shit, do you, boy? Got no oars, got no idea." Pressy leaned down. "That cold steel slides inside them boys, and they open up like cans. You know what they say?"

Stu said nothing.

The man raised the skinless catfish. "I just set it free," he said. "Didn't I? I fixed the worst problem it had—being a catfish. That's why it nosed the bait, you know? Same reason you come, too, full of sickness."

He tossed the cleaned meat into a bucket and then took his long stick from where it leaned against the tree. He hefted it and then held it out above Stu's boat.

"'God!' is what they say." He waved the stick over Stu. "'Oh, God!'"

Vernon said that if a buzzard breathed on you, you'd die. But if you could pull out just one tail feather without getting breathed on, why then you'd live forever.

Stu and Vernon acted dead in the back yard one day, lying still and all sprawled around—same way dead things do, like they didn't care what they looked like. Ants crawled on them, but they didn't move. Bees buzzed in their ears, and angry voices came from the house, but they weren't afraid. There were buzzards high in the sky.

"When it comes down," Vernon said, "it'll cover the sun. It'll lean over you, and you'll see the lice in its feathers. First thing, it'll want to peck your eyes, so you got to jump up before it breathes on you, jump up and grab it by the neck. While you're doing that, I'll pull out the feather. It'll beat you with its wings and open its mouth to scream, but you got to hold on."

They were dead a long time, but the buzzards never came. Vernon said it was because they didn't have the right smell. So they walked along the road until they found a dead possum. Vernon told Stu to touch it and wipe the stink on both of them. "Come on," he said, "you're the one's got the touch."

Pressy raised his stick under the willow and pointed it where the sky should be. "'God,'" he said. Then he lowered the stick and jabbed it into the mud. "'Oh God!'

"You know why they say that?" The man lifted his stick above Stu. "Course you don't know why. Come on up here, boy," Pressy said. "Grab onto this stick. I'm gonna fix you. Come on, little trap stealer.

See them fish heads? They ain't worried no more about the cold world coming inside. They know all about it and are praising right there on that tree. When you get stabbed, now, don't you call out 'God!' Don't you try to hold it off with that. You just let it in."

Stu raised his palm to push the man's stick away, but Pressy held it above the boat just out of reach. Cicadas chanted in the high branches where the sunlight was bright. Stu smelled salt, and he saw that he was moving before the tide.

Pressy crunched cicada husks as he walked along the waterside. New things had grown inside until the backs of the old things split open and the new things pulled their legs out of the old legs and pulled their faces out from behind the old faces. Then the new things wriggled out of their old selves. Their new wings unfolded and they flew up into the high branches and filled the tree with song.

"Come on, boy," the man said.

Stu's boat parted the willow curtain, and he squinted in the evening sunlight. All that was left under the tree were empty husks. So was the world back and forth? Or was it on and on? He tried to grab the muddy end of Pressy's stick, but it slid from his grip and left him with nothing but mud in his palm.

The willow curtain closed on Pressy, but his laugh came from the shadows. "And don't come back," he said, "because I'm waiting for you."

The current pushed Stu back the way he came—past the dead end at Hubble Avenue, and then past the one at Pearl Street. A few stars came out, and soon he was near his own yard. He heard his father calling him, and then his mother's voice joined in, and the two made a strange high and low like a foghorn.

Stu rode the current, waiting for the breeze that would push him into the reeds by his yard. He heard his parents calling, but he said nothing.

He had seen them like this before: where the back splits open, but something goes wrong and the new thing dies halfway out. He heard his mother and father calling him, but he said nothing because the only things he knew were things he couldn't understand.

Hollowed Be
Thy Name

At first, it was only a moan, as if the old school building had come alive and was groaning from the stiffness of a century. It was not even a sound, really, but more a vibration Stu felt in his shoes and in his spine. The pitch climbed upward through his body and stretched itself into a screech that seemed to come, somehow, from the back of his neck.

The teacher hurried to put the model of the atom away, but the crank that spun the electrons kept catching on the edge of the science box.

Students clenched their teeth when the scream blossomed, finally, into the wide open wail of the siren.

Frustrated and frantic, the teacher shouted, "Two lines! Hurry!"

Quickly as he could, Stu pushed back from his desk and got in line. Still, he was last. Always, he was last. Kids shoved. Some of them whined along with the siren, their lips curled into snarls. They pushed him to the back of the line, where Linda stood. She crimped her hand into a claw. Her mouth went, "Raa!" But there was no sound except siren.

When they played together after school, her dog would growl when she clawed like that. He would growl like evil and go for her, snarling. Linda would run. Afraid but laughing, she ran, and Stu ran with her. Then, safe in their favorite tree, they grinned down at the beast. Wasn't she afraid to have a dog that bit? he wanted to know.

She was not afraid, she said. You can't really *be* scared, when you're afraid all the time. Then she told him about the men who came to her house and the noises she heard that were like hurt. But it was okay. Her mom was okay. And so, no, she was not afraid of her dog.

The teacher left the atom clinging to the side of its box and shooed students into the hall. She touched kids on their shoulders, moving them along. She was old. Her knuckles were swollen, and the fingers went out wrong from them. Everybody crowded together, squeezing toward the stairs until the lines from all the classrooms had melted into a mass. Stu stopped at the top of the steps and let students from other classes pour past him and down. Linda stood there too, smiling and clawing her hand as if she didn't care one bit that the sky could explode at any moment and radiation could fall on them like rain.

At breakfast, Stu had asked his mother what he should do if the siren sounded after school before he had a chance to get to the bus. The newspaper in front of his father's face showed a map with arrows flying to the United States. Wherever an arrow pointed, a gray mushroom grew. You never knew when it would happen, but you knew that there would be sirens.

His mother was busy. He was the last of the brothers to leave the house every morning, and by then she was frazzled. She tucked stray hair behind her ear and turned toward his father. "Don't worry about dying in the bomb," his mother said. "When God wants, you go. That's all."

The newspaper dropped just far enough to show his father's eyes. The brows pitched together in a "V" and one eye narrowed. "Don't make it worse than it already is, Edna."

She shrugged. "God's will," she said.

"Son," said his father. "When that siren goes off, you head someplace with a fallout shelter or at least head for a basement somewhere."

His mother shook her head. "What you ought to do," she said, "is stand up and take what God's got to give."

The paper sighed. His father reached behind his ear and turned the wheel on his hearing aid. "You want war with me, Edna?"

His mother and father stared at each other. Stu knew all about their war—it hung over them like a sky, and it could go from words to worse without any warning at all.

Stu eased into the stream of students and let himself be pulled down the stairs. At the bottom, he grabbed the post and stood there while kids bumped past him. Big lights hung from long chains there in the first floor hallway. His teacher was at the front door, and her mouth was going, "Hurry! No running. No running. Hurry!"

Linda knelt on the steps above him and looked through the bars in the railing like a prisoner. "Save me," her mouth went.

When they were in the tree, hiding from the dog, she had shown Stu how to do it. She had pulled him close and made him put his arms around her. She was small for sixth grade, and she smelled of kerosene, but it felt good holding her, even though it was not good. Linda was not good. Stu's mother had said. Still, something pulled him more than fear pushed, and holding her, Stu had trembled so badly that he thought he might fall from the tree and into the teeth of the beast.

When the dog was gone one day, Linda took Stu into the cave of blackberry vines and tried to show him the meaning of life. It was under her dress, she had said, between her legs. She had heard her mother say that was where it was—the meaning of life. All Stu saw, though, was confusion. He had only brothers and could make no sense of what she tried to show him there amid the vines and the shadows.

When he went home for dinner that night, his mother met him at the back door with a broom in her hand. She made him stand on the porch while she swept him—first his knees and then his bottom, which she hit so hard that, if he hadn't known he was special to God, Stu might have thought she was spanking him.

She set the broom aside and picked twigs out of Stu's hair. "You spend too much time in those woods," she said, "crawling around like an animal with that . . . girl."

His mother put her hands on Stu's shoulders and steered him into the kitchen. Dinner was on the stove, and his father was at the table. The paper in front of him held yet another map, another crop of mushrooms.

Stu asked them then, just to see how wrong they could be, if they knew what the meaning of life was.

His father grunted from behind the paper.

"Why," his mother squinted, "God."

Stu stared at her. In his mind there was only confusion and the smell of blackberry vines.

"Life's got no meaning," said the voice behind the paper. "Read the news for a week, and you'll figure that out."

Linda stared at him through the railing, her hands prison-gripping the bars, her mouth going, "Save me. Save me."

When Stu passed the county jail on the way from the bus to school in the mornings, men in denim sometimes stuck their fingers through the wired windows. They said things that Stu did not listen to. He just walked through the alley to Market Street, where the sun was coming up and where the yellow sign with its upside down triangles hung above the jail's front door. "Fallout Shelter," it said. When it was time, when you knew the bombs were coming, you could commit some sort of crime and be saved.

Now, the teacher's back was toward him. She was looking out the front door, pointing crookedly, and counting kids as they lined up on the playground. The trees out there were like mushroom clouds, and the ground was red with leaves. Usually, they would turn at the post where Stu stood and head down the stairs to the basement movie room. But now the basement door was closed, and kids hurried past, walking stiff-legged to keep from running. Some of them were smiling. The teacher nodded and touched their shoulders and then sent them outside to stand under the sky.

Stu could smell the basement—cool and clean like a sidewalk after rain. His father had sandbagged the windows of their basement at home because an article in the paper said that it would cut the radiation by sixty percent. The whole world could catch fire, but in a basement you would survive.

"Save me," Linda's mouth went.

After the Lord's Prayer and the Pledge of Allegiance this morning, the teacher had pinched the crank between her twisted fingers and spun the electrons into a blur. "What," she had wanted to know, "are atoms made of?"

Bobby Klein raised his hand. "Electrons, neutrons, protrons."

"Pro*tons*," the teacher had said, "yes."

But a substitute teacher had told them once that atoms were

mostly nothing. Mostly space. They were like bicycle wheels when the spokes blur into a gray that seemed almost solid but wasn't.

Stu understood. He had read the entire Bible, and so he knew that when God made the world, He did not fill the void. He only gave the void a shape. And so Stu raised his hand in class and said that he knew what atom bombs did.

"Oh?" said the teacher.

"They break atoms," he said, "and that way nothing has no shape anymore, and so it gets turned loose on the world again."

Something tugged the corners of the teacher's mouth downward. "Two negatives make a positive," she had said. "You mean nothing has *any* shape anymore."

And now the teacher was standing by the front doors, her mouth full of siren. She turned her back to count kids, and Stu pulled open the basement door. The smell of concrete was strong. Linda was next to him, and when Stu squeezed through, she followed. By the time they were at the bottom of the steps, the door had closed above them, and the siren seemed far away. They walked along the dim hall, their shoes tapping on the concrete, until they came to the movie room. Stu pulled open the door. Except for the red glow of the exit sign, it was dark in there. Row after row of folding chairs filled the place. Always, Stu and Linda were among the last to get in, but now they were first.

She came close and put her arms around him. "Save me," she whispered.

He put his arms around her and could feel the bone in her back and the softer smoothness on either side. She was trembling.

He squeezed her, and in the red glow of the exit sign, she pressed the meaning of life against him. "Ahh," she said, and it was a sound like in the middle of "god." His mother had told him. It was wrong to touch girls, to hold them to you, but Stu prayed to his Father who was in heaven. Hollowed was his name, like an atom, where nothing had a shape. God was a space, like a basement, where you could make a nest and be saved. It was a place where grown-ups were not at war, teachers were not wrong, countries were not stupid.

Stu and Linda held each other in the red air until the siren stopped.

Far away, voices called their names. Then they heard footsteps on the stairs and then footsteps coming down the hall. The doorknob turned. A shaft of white light cut the air, and, suddenly, Linda was out of his arms, sitting in a chair next to where he stood.

The overheads flickered on. "What are you two doing?" It was the teacher. Her voice was part anger and part relief. "It's a *fire drill*," she said. "You would have been burned alive down here. Now get out and line up with the rest."

Stu felt his face go red. He walked out of the movie room and into the hall. Linda followed. They climbed the stairs, and Stu stopped at the big doors. The kids outside were standing in crooked lines.

"Next time," the teacher said, "do as you're told."

The teacher's hand touched his shoulder, and Stu and Linda headed down the front steps of the building. Kids pointed at them and grinned. They descended to the playground and took their places in line.

They stood there with the good and the obedient outside a building that was not on fire but under a sky that could explode at any moment.

Edna
and Coy

She heard the old fool pull into the driveway. Well, how was she gonna miss him? A hundred times she had told him to get his truck fixed, but he never would do it. He couldn't hear was the problem, and on top of that, he wouldn't admit that he couldn't hear. So what did he care if he drove something that sounded like a stuck pig?

His dogs were gone again. Edna could tell that just by the sound of things. Three thousand dollars worth of blue tick mixes running loose in the woods somewhere. It wasn't such a big number any-more—three thousand dollars—unless you were a pulp wooder and didn't make but eight or nine a year. Oh, a young man might make more than that, but, then again, young men these days had better sense than to be pulp wooders.

But twenty years ago, when she first met him, pulping was the thing to do. All you needed was a chain saw and enough courage to use it. Lots of men were afraid of such saws, and good reason, too. Many's a one sawed through a boot top or cut a branch that sprung back and snapped him into the next world. But not Coy. He was strong. A chain saw was nothing more to him than a tamed scream at the end of his big arms. In five minutes, he could bring down a tree it'd take two men with a cross-cut an hour to fell. That was back before the big woods were cut over. Back when you could get three loads of pulp wood from the laps of a single tree. It seemed to her that back in those days everywhere Coy turned another tree was coming down and then there was Coy standing over the carcass cut-ting off the money and loading it onto his truck. And now, all these years later, his forearms were still bigger than most men's calves, but they were laced with varicose veins, and sometimes they hurt so bad that Coy couldn't cut. Even though it was only planted pine not much bigger around than her leg, he still couldn't cut. He never said anything. But he'd come home with half a load or less, and she'd know.

When they were young, though, their wood lot was always stacked high, and as far as they knew, they were rich. First thing Coy always wanted were good dogs. Blue tick and red bone—howlers and criers. On nights when the moon shined down on mist that filled the marshes, the two of them would load the dogs into the truck and drive out into the country. They'd turn the dogs loose and sit in the truck listening to the howls echo through the woods. It put the hair up on Edna's arms it was so beautiful and eerie. Seemed like it was the sound of their two spirits spinning through those trees, chasing after what they knew they needed while their bodies stayed in the truck doing what bodies could think to do.

Then came marriage and miscarriages and still births and, finally, three boys. Coy went without her after that, he and his buddies. They weren't satisfied to sit in the truck and listen but had to get liquored up, put pistols in their pockets. They'd light out through the woods chasing sounds. Sometimes they found the dogs around a tree. She never understood why they had to carry it that far, why they wanted to see the coon's eyes shine in their flashlight beams, why they'd shoot at it until it fell, or until it died in the arms of the tree. Sometimes Coy told her about coons that seemed to disappear, right out of the tree, somehow, so that the dogs had to be tied up and dragged back to the truck.

She thought that was God's work.

And sometimes, of course, they'd lose the dogs. There'd be a howling out there, but liquor and the hollows confused the sounds. The men would wander into briars or swamps until, finally, they'd quit. Coy'd come home then, alone, and she'd be able to tell whether he was mad from the way he closed the truck door and by the sound of his steps on the back porch. If the dogs had struck hard and tracked fast, they might have just left the men behind. He'd be excited then and his steps would be quick and loud—what a coon, strong and smart. You could lose dogs over an animal like that and feel proud.

But if the dogs had wandered and fretted and never struck hard but wouldn't come when they blew the horn, why, he'd be mad. His steps would be slower and quiet like he was trying to sneak up on something. He'd tell her that he didn't care if he never found them dogs again. She'd remind him what they cost, but he'd swear and say it was a small amount to lose to be rid of something that couldn't do what it was put on Earth to do.

But anymore, it was harder to tell how he felt by the sound of his steps because he didn't step so much now as shuffle. She heard him head toward the shed to put away his pistol and take off his boots. He ought not hunt was what she thought. For one thing, there was nobody to go with him. The boys wanted no part of it, and old Mr. Logan was in the White Oak Nursing Home now, because it got to the point where he had forgotten how to get home from the store. And there was no way that Edna would go into the woods with Coy. Not now, not with three teenage boys to take care of. No, she had long ago given up foolishness like that. No, God had turned against Coy, and so he went by himself, and it wasn't safe. Pulping had worn him out and made an old man of him before he was fifty. Time was you had to worry about bears and even panthers. Thank goodness those times were gone, but it wasn't really any safer now because God was a whole lot fiercer than wild animals.

She knew all she needed to about that. Her first babies taught her how to mother the dead. And then, when the three boys came along, it was hard to believe they'd live. Accidents and illness were everywhere, and poor Stuart, the sickest one, surprised her by surviving to be a teenager. He had been sick enough to take the measure of God, and she saw that Stu could fix what God broke, heal what God made un-whole.

But when it came to Coy, it was plain as chestnuts to Edna—by a certain age most people ought to admit they can't catch what runs in the woods. They ought to stay home, lock the door, pray. Ought to let young people be the ones who fight the Lord. But the older you got, it seemed, the more often you had to look Him in the eye.

Coy stepped into the kitchen and stood there in his dirty socks looking at her across the room.

"Well?" she said.

He turned away and got a drink of water. He was chainsaw-deaf and not wearing his hearing aid, as usual.

"Where are they this time?"

"There ain't no woods nomore," he said. "You can drive all the way to the next county and pass nothing but saplings smaller around than a dog's waist. Take a weasel to find a coon in such a mess as that. I don't even know why I keep dogs anymore."

"Well," she said, "sounds like you don't."

"Not even hardly a tree big enough to hold a good sized coon."

"You ought to sell those dogs."

"Down in the south of the county, right there by the river, there's still some woods, but they've cut over parts of it, so you walk a while and then you come to a thicket can't a gnat get through. And if they do strike in there, why, you can't halfway hear because the sound won't carry through a mess like that."

No, she thought, the old fool's ears were twice as big as when he was young, but the bigger they got, the worse they worked.

"Better get some sleep," she said. "So you can hunt them tomorrow."

"I'm going to bed," he said, and she nodded.

But he didn't get up early the next morning and drive the dirt roads looking for the dogs. And he didn't go out in the evening either. All he did was fool around in his shed with the boys, filling boxes, and trash bags. When he came in to wash his hands for supper, she stood right next to him and looked him in the eye. "It's good money," she said, "just starving to death out there."

He turned from the sink and said, "Huh?"

It was bad being deaf, but she could see that it had its uses.

After the kids went to bed, they sat in the living room watching her shows. He stared at the TV, but she didn't think he was really watching. He never once asked her to run the volume up, and he only seemed to come to himself during commercials when girls in bathing suits flashed across the screen.

"Get up," she wanted to tell him. "What sort of a man sits there and watches shows like he's in a trance?"

In the middle of "Hitchcock," he pushed himself out of his chair.

"I'm going to bed," he said, like he had lost some sort of battle he was fighting. She watched him slouch up the steps, and then she turned back to her show. It was no use trusting an old man. Once they couldn't work anymore they couldn't stand up for themselves, couldn't spit a single spit in God's eye. No, she was half tempted to go find those dogs herself—find them and sell them.

He didn't go out looking the next morning either. And at supper he wouldn't say anything to her but, "Huh?" After dinner, he sat there in the living room all evening while the room got dark. He didn't even hear the phone when it rang.

The young man on the other end said he had found some dogs at his place and the tags had this number on it.

"Yes," Edna said. "Let me have you talk to my husband."

She held the phone out toward Coy and he groaned coming out of the chair. "Where?" he said into the phone. "Wait a minute."

He gave the phone back to her. "I can't tell what he's saying."

She got the location and hung up. "Let's go," she said.

He filled two bowls with food and put them in the back of the truck next to the dog cages. "You drive," he told her.

She headed them down the Coxe Road, the truck screaming all the way. They turned off onto the Watson Road, which was dirt, and then off onto a farm road, which was just two ruts through the woods. The road climbed a hill and wound between white oaks into the driveway of an old log house.

"I know this place," Coy said. "There was a bear tore the convertible top off a man's car lived here. Must've been twenty years ago. Fool left food in the back seat and the bear went right through the top. Fellow ran him off by throwing stones. Saved some of the food, but the roof of that car was nothing but rags."

The first thing that came to greet them was a black lab. It looked like a shadow in their headlights. The dog lifted its leg and marked their tires.

"That dog's no kind of use around here," Coy said.

Next came three dogs, their tails between their legs. Edna recognized the blue tick markings, but the dogs seemed smaller, somehow, than their dogs. They bred them down, these days. Coy had explained it to her. They mixed in bird dog so they could hunt better in brush. He didn't like it. Little dogs for chasing little coons through little woods. Not a thing to be proud of, but it was all you could do anymore since the world had gotten so small and so filled up with children and pups and saplings that there was hardly any place for something full grown. The lab jumped back and forth, bowing to play. One of the mixes wrestled with it.

"Useless," Coy mumbled.

Next came a young man in short pants. He had a little goatee and a big smile.

Edna smiled back at the boy and looked over at Coy. He didn't seem to notice the kid, though. He was looking straight ahead, and she followed his eyes to a girl in short pants and wearing the top to a bathing suit. She stopped to pet the dogs, which gathered around and followed her to the truck.

The boy was talking a streak about how they had seen the dogs yesterday at twilight, but that they wouldn't come out of the woods. Then this evening they must have gotten the courage to come up and make friends with Jessie (which Edna didn't know was the lab or the girl). And then the boy had managed to read the number on one of their collars and so he had called, and goodness they really loved the sound coon dogs made in the woods at night, but Laura didn't like the idea of killing coons. (So Edna knew, then, that Laura most likely was the girl.) The boy said he had told Laura that lots of times hunters didn't even bother to follow the dogs but just let them run to hear their music and then called them back and went home. Sometimes, though, the dogs wouldn't come and so they left them, knowing they would go someplace or other when they got hungry enough. Just good thing they found somebody honest this time, the boy said. Yes, Jessie and Laura both liked them just fine. Real nice coon dogs.

Edna had never heard the like. This boy was some sort of Yankee, or maybe he was just from some big city, but either way he was one of those people that comes at you talking and leaves you talking and never shuts up enough to let the world catch its breath. Nice coon dogs. What foolishness. The young could have it worse than the old. A good coon dog didn't care a thing about people except for food. No, all a coon dog cared about was the woods and what his nose could take him to.

"Well they sure are friendly," the boy was saying, "and pretty—they sing fine at night. Why, with the moon full and . . ."

She turned to Coy. "You going to feed them?"

"Ain't mine," he said.

"What?" she said.

He looked her straight in the eye and said, "Huh?"

How long? she wondered. How long before Coy wouldn't be able to find his way home from the store either? She had fallen in love with this man. She had wanted to spend her life with him, and she had. She had lived with him until now it seemed like God had most of what was left and there was hardly a thing for her.

She got out of the truck and put the food bowls on the ground. The dogs didn't even bother to smell what was there.

"Oh," said the boy. "Laura made bacon and eggs for them a little while ago.

"They sure were hungry," said Laura, and she smiled sweetly at the dogs.

"Let's go," Coy said. "Get in the truck."

"I'll help you load them up," the boy said, and he bent down and picked up one of the dogs. It wasn't like Coy did it. Coy picked dogs up by the scruff of the neck and the skin of their rumps, and he pitched them like bales of hay. But this boy put his arms underneath and held the dog the way Jesus holds the lamb in that picture. Edna didn't open the cage door. She just looked at the boy with his arms under the dog, and the dog looking surprised and yet somehow content, like it didn't care if it never ran in the woods again.

Coy leaned out the window. "That's not mine," he said.

"But, it's got your number right here on the collar," the boy said.

Coy squinted. "What do you reckon you'd do, short pants, if a bear came through the roof of *your* car?"

The boy cocked his head and smiled. "Huh?" he said.

Edna was about to argue with the old fool, right there in front of strangers—this was good money here, their money, but it'd do no good to argue with him now—she knew that—not with his foolish mind made up. She put the bowls back in the truck and got behind the wheel. They could come back another day, or she could. The truck screamed when she started it. Then she turned around and drove down the ruts, leaving the boy and girl standing there in a swirl of dogs and exhaust.

When they turned onto the Watson Road, Edna said, "Have you gone completely crazy or are you only halfway there? That's three thousand dollars worth of dogs."

"Not mine," he said.

They were a mile down the road, just crossing White Oak Creek, when he told her to pull over and shut the truck off. The trees were still big along the creek because the law wouldn't let loggers cut there. The darkness was deep, and it smelled cool and rich.

"Now," he said, and his head cocked like he heard something. "Those are my dogs."

She listened to the breeze high in the leaves and to the water hissing across rocks in the creek. If there had been some hounds sounding it would have been like the old days—back when she and Coy thought that the woods would go on forever and that they would go on forever, too, back when a whole forest of tall trees held the stars higher in the sky.

"Twenty years," he said. "It's not a long time to kill every bear and cut every tree."

She nodded. "It's enough."

They stared through the windshield at the darkness. "I done my share of it," Coy said. "Must of cut a million trees, but I can't work no more, Edna. I can't hear the dogs no more. And there ain't no woods no more. Only little patches, like this, to make a man miserable."

Well, it was true. He couldn't work, and he knew he couldn't work. She started the truck and pulled onto the road. The woods glided past, and she could smell the soft, rich smells.

"Can you hear 'em?" Coy said.

She did not look at him. She didn't need to. He was familiar to her in every wrinkle and pain. He was hers to have and to hold, but it was as if her hand had closed on sand, and he was lost forever.

The leaves were turning yellow already. Another winter would be on them, soon. Well, so what if he didn't want his own dogs? That was fine with her, but to leave them at some stranger's house, well, it was foolish—a waste of money they didn't have. Just when she thought she knew the exact shape of the old fool's foolishness, here it had gone and taken on a new shape, and now she was going to have to figure him out all over again.

Tomorrow. She would come back tomorrow and gather them up and sell them.

"Do you hear?" he said.

She stopped at the intersection with Coxe Road. The truck screamed, and the cicadas were working themselves up into crazy rhythms. No, she did not hear old hounds running through the woods of a deaf man's memory. She did not hear their mournful cries when they struck trail, did not hear how their music got sadder and more desperate the closer they got to what they wanted. What was it, she had always wondered, that drove them to chase after things that made them so sad?

Coy was leaning his head out the window, listening. He was out there somewhere, spinning on ahead of her. She wanted to cry his name, wanted to say "Coy, what's happening to you? Where is the man I used to know?" She wanted to bring him back to her, wanted to have him and hold him, but getting what you wanted—holding it in your hand or in your heart—getting what you wanted only meant that it was going to be gone from your life forever.

She pulled out onto the highway. Countless times she had driven this way, but all of a sudden she wasn't sure if the road wound left or right up ahead. Left, she thought it went left, but she slowed down anyway just in case God had another surprise for her up ahead.

MIA

When JoAnna came into the bar on that Halloween night dressed up like a dead Viet Cong, Stu decided right away that he had no desire at all to find out why. His wife was wearing black shorts that were slit up the sides like a loincloth, and the handle of a bayonet stuck out from between her breasts. Her face was painted yellow and the corners of her eyes were drawn up into points with eyeliner. Blood crusted the front of her black shirt, and blood traced paths down the insides of her thighs. She was supposed to have been raped and killed, Stu realized, and he hated that he had figured out even that much.

Her crowd sat at a table not far from Stu's. She sprawled in her seat, her legs spread and her head lolling as much like a dead person's as she could make it and still drink beer. A guy dressed in olive drab reached over and pulled the bayonet from her chest. JoAnna opened her eyes and roused herself as if resurrected. The guy waggled the retractable rubber blade at her. Then he plunged it in again, and JoAnna writhed and died again. They played this game several times until JoAnna said she was satisfied and asked for a cigarette. The table laughed and they all decided they needed more drinks.

JoAnna was scanning for the waitress when she saw him. At least he thought she saw him. Her eyes locked onto his, and her forehead wrinkled as if she were having trouble reading a map. He recognized the look, and he groaned.

Stu's friend Brody leaned across the table, and Stu simply nodded in JoAnna's direction. Brody turned around. She held both of them with her eyes, dark and deep. Stu felt himself emptying into her just as he always had. Slowly, she slid the knife out from between her breasts, and just as slowly, she stabbed herself again and died back into her group.

After she had turned away, Brody shook his head. "Bitch," he said. Stu couldn't tell exactly who she was with. That was JoAnna's way. She wasn't with men; men were with her. Whoever she turned those eyes on thought he was the one, and once he had fallen in, he would never be free.

Two guys in her group were in costume. One was done up like a POW—his face made to seem emaciated and his clothes dingy and baggy. The other was the guy with the olive-drab coveralls and the plastic gun. He was fat around the middle, but his head and neck were oddly skinny. He was handsome, though, and tall. Stu figured he was the one. Power attracted power. Even raped and murdered, JoAnna would be more than a match for this make-believe GI.

"Ain't nobody like her," Stu said.

"Well, good," said Brody. He stood up. "I need something for the head."

Stu followed him out. They crunched across the gravel of the parking lot to the far end, where a single streetlight struggled to shine through the kudzu that was slowly engulfing it. There had been no killing frost yet, so the tendrils of the vines still clung like boa constrictors, and the growing tips still unrolled trails of leaves that plunged whatever they covered into a green gloom. Trees killed by kudzu loomed like shrouded skeletons, and beneath them—kudzu caves. Brody ducked into one and Stu followed. Beer cans and wine bottles littered the little space. The ground was covered with leaves that smelled like wet paper bags. Brody sat on a rusty paint can and pulled a bone from his shirt pocket. He lit it, took a drag, and passed it to Stu, who was sitting on the edge of an old tire.

Time slowed. Stu liked this best about pot—it held out the hope that you might prevent the future. The street light shone through the kudzu leaves. At its center, the light was brilliant white, but it faded to a deep green in just a few feet. It was like looking at a white hot weld through the dark green glass of a welding mask—a smoky, molten place of shadows with fire at its center.

Stu pulled more marijuana into his lungs. Time thickened like slag. How beautiful it was to watch the arc, hot as the sun, liquid and shimmering. And then in an instant, the metal cooled and was solid, harder than steel. When you flipped your mask up and looked at the weld in the light of day, it was gray and hard, though tiny waves were still frozen in it. You wondered then if it was solid at all until you touched it, and then you had to believe that it had never been liquid and that everything you saw through the welding glass had been a smoky dream.

"Where you at?" Brody said. He was holding what was left of the joint. Green light filtered down around them. Frost would come soon, and when it did, all those leaves would shrivel up into little brown balls.

"Come on." Brody flicked the roach away. "You need a drink. She got nothing on you."

Back inside, JoAnna danced. The jukebox was full of Motown, and JoAnna bopped and swirled, the bayonet still in her chest. "Can't kill the VC," Stu heard her sing, "never enough, no, not ever enough." She spun, and Stu grew dizzy. "Kill us," she said, "and we come back."

A month ago, his parents had received a letter that was sorry to inform them that their son Vernon was missing in Southeast Asia. Stu tried not to think about it. Vernon was only two years older, and Stu preferred to picture his brother holed up in some whorehouse doing his best to stop time, too, and let the war fight itself.

JoAnna twisted.

"Let's go," Stu said.

"Stay," said Brody. "You'll be better off if you see what she is."

Then she faced Stu and made the room spin while she stood still in the center.

Marriage, it turned out, hadn't fixed a thing. JoAnna was pregnant by somebody else when Stu married her. She went with the "best guys," as she said. Always, she wanted to show that family of hers how much she was worth. But when she turned up pregnant, her best guy finally heard his country's call and decided that his duty was in Vietnam. And there she was with no place to land.

When she began to talk to Stu, he was flattered. It felt to him as if he had finally grown into clothes that had been bought too big. He didn't even mind that she was pregnant. The child had brought her to him, and he was grateful for it.

JoAnna only nodded when the Justice of the Peace asked if she would take Stu as her husband, so he repeated the question. She looked at Stu, then, her eyes as bottomless as ever, and said, "I will."

Soon after they graduated from high school, they moved into a little rented house, and gravity began to pull down the corners of JoAnna's mouth. When Stu came home from work, her forehead wrinkled as if she was trying to place just who he was.

"Zombie bop," JoAnna crooned in the bar. She whirled from one partner to another. "Zombie wants you," she would say, and another guy would rise from his seat or leave his partner to dance with the dead VC.

They had only been married a couple weeks when JoAnna woke in the middle of the night with cramps so bad that she couldn't stand. Stu was terrified. By the time he got her to the hospital, she was already drifting away. And when she came home a few days later, it was as if she had lost who she was and couldn't find anything else to take its place. Stu was full of questions. He wanted to know what they had done with it. Had it been a child at all, or just a sort of idea with blood? He tried to ask, but JoAnna's forehead wrinkled, and he would not have been surprised at that moment if she had demanded to know exactly who he was.

He worked longer hours, hoping the extra money would convince her that she had not made a mistake by marrying him. He squeezed the welding gun like a weapon, beating production every shift. In the mornings, lying next to his wife, he was ashamed to touch her sometimes because his hand was cramped into a claw.

But he was a good welder, the best. He could put furniture together on the jig and weld it up without really waking. He could make settees and dream JoAnna onto them all at the same time. He had learned to be this good, and he still had hope that learning could take you someplace you wanted to go. She looked fine, JoAnna did—wide-eyed, long-necked, perfect JoAnna, his wife. He had trouble believing it. "My wife," he kept saying to himself, its half rhyme tolling like a bell inside his mask. The wire-mesh seats would put crosshatches on her thighs. His hand felt their ridges even through thick welding gloves, and he felt the flesh smooth out high on her rear where the seat would not touch. The tingle he got shot right into his skin. He could feel her on the underside of his forearm where the skin was so sensitive and so smooth. Sometimes the cuff of his glove touched him there and gave him chills. She was fine, she would always be there, seated in his mind, almost welded in place. But when he flipped his mask up and looked down, he saw that the white hot welding wire had burned into his arm, cauterizing the flesh as it penetrated. There was just this wire disappearing into him as if he were plugged in.

The VC's thighs were bloody. She touched Stu's shoulder, and he looked into eyes that seemed too deep to be alive. Her hand slid from his shoulder and closed around his hand. She leaned toward the dance floor, pulling his arm out straight. He felt himself rising and falling into that place again.

He was amazed that the wire had not hurt much. When the foreman saw it, the hole was angry around the edges. "How deep it go in?" he asked.

"Inch, maybe."

The man frowned. "Goddamn, son. Most people who touch a hot wire pull away a little quicker than that."

Stu shrugged. What could he say? That he had been dreaming of his wife? That he had been planning to crawl up on that settee and satisfy a thirst that was all the more intense because he couldn't believe that he was actually allowed to drink? He smiled.

"You trying to hurt yourself?"

"No, sir. I was thinking about my wife."

The foreman frowned more deeply this time. "I got a safety record to think about, son," he said. He walked Stu to the time clock and punched his card. "Come back," he said, "when you're better."

He was falling. He was on his feet and falling into JoAnna. But the GI was there, his fat middle bulging and his thin neck coming up through his collar like a periscope. He put his gun to JoAnna's throat.

Her fingers tightened on Stu's hand. "Whose side are you on?" she said to Stu. "Bad as the rest?"

"Nobody ain't on the dead's side," the GI said. He pressed the gun into the flesh of her neck. Her head tilted back, and she dropped Stu's hand. The GI cupped her chin in his palm and squeezed her cheeks with his fingers until her mouth opened.

"Come on," she said.

"I seen what people get," the GI said. "And I'm good for giving it."

Getting hurt that day hadn't seemed all bad. Off early, he was going to have time for JoAnna, he thought, and it was dusk. He rarely got to see dusk working second shift. A slit of gray cut the western sky and some stars were out in the east. Troubles on earth would be just small points of light in those distant skies. So he had walked slowly, enjoying the late summer evening and grateful to have a place to go when there was trouble. But when he pulled on the screen door of their little house, he found it was locked. No one came when he knocked, so he headed through the side yard, where the apple tree had dropped its fruit a few weeks before. With every step, Stu squashed something, and a smell rose from his shoes—part cider, part garbage.

When he reached for the back door, the knob turned from inside and the door swung open. A cop stepped into the doorway. He was tall, dressed in black, and he stood there with his arms bowing around his belt, which was heavy with handcuffs, radio, club, gun. He looked down at Stu, but then he seemed to look right through him.

The man cleared his throat, and Stu stood flat-footed waiting to hear, but the cop stepped past him without a word. He walked through the side yard—must have squashed a dozen apples but never seemed to miss a step. He just kept on to the sidewalk, his middle jiggling unnaturally. Then he turned up the street and was gone.

Stu went in, feeling as if he had walked into something he had no ticket for. JoAnna was on the couch in her bathrobe. The only light came from the TV, where a detective of some sort smiled. The room was blue with that light, and there were shadows like those you could see through the deep dark of the welding glass.

JoAnna turned toward him. Her breasts pressed against the fabric of the robe. "What're you doing home?"

"Hurt myself," he said and held out his arm.

"Ouch," said JoAnna, instantly making the small hole seem even smaller. "Want a Band-Aid?"

"Not bleeding," Stu said. "Who was that?"

"That job of yours is too dangerous," she said. "Maybe you ought to move up and get a good job."

"Who was it?"

JoAnna's nose wrinkled and she looked down at his feet. "Phew," she said.

"Rotten apples," Stu said. "Who was it?"

Her forehead wrinkled. "A cop," she said. "I heard a prowler and called."

Stu turned away instinctively—the way you did when someone else's arc lit up the factory: you threw up your hand to shade your eyes, and you turned away. Why, then, hadn't the cop wanted to know who he was, there at the backdoor?

The GI blindfolded the VC and, with his gun pressed into the back of her neck, paraded her around the bar. "Interrogate her," he told them. "Ask her how come she kills our boys. Go ahead, ask."

After that day at the house, Stu lost himself in his work. At the end of every shift, his snot was black and his arms were pitted with small burns. He welded such long hours that his eyes hurt. And after work he did not want to go home. If he'd had the stamina, he would have stayed behind the mask constantly—smoke and fire and money were the closest things to happiness he could imagine. Most nights he went to his parents' house for dinner. It was comfortable being among people who knew even less than he did. He envied them, but his mother surprised him one night.

"I've lost babies."

His father winced, and Stu felt a past open up beneath him.

Stu's mother never talked about herself. She lived like someone sitting alone in a waiting room putting up with what you put up with before you moved on to important things. Her hair was drab, her eyebrows invisible. She wore dresses that gave her no particular shape. There was almost nothing about her: not beauty, not ugliness, barely enough to make a self.

"I used to go to church," she said, "until I had my first miscarriage.

Preacher wanted to hear all about it, so I told him about the boy and about how much in love I was and about how I wanted the baby and then how it got pulled away, by what I didn't know. And when I finished, he looked down at me and said that I should ask forgiveness.

"I was young, but I looked him in the eye and didn't say a word.

"He frowned down trying to scare me, but I didn't scare because, you know, even at that age I had seen the shape of God. Next Sunday, I went dressed in black because I was mourning. That preacher came down the line giving everybody a wafer and saying they ought to take it and eat it because it was the body of Christ that was given for them and that it would wash away their sins and so forth, but when he got to me, he stopped. Then he looked past me and started to move on to the next person.

"Well, I reached out and grabbed a wafer. Preacher frowned down at me, and you know what I said? I said, 'Christ didn't have a body because he never give it to a woman.' That's what I said. Then I ate that wafer and smacked my lips."

His mother laughed a single "ha!" like a sneeze. "You go a little crazy when you lose a baby," she said. "It's like you're afraid you did something wrong. She'll come around."

But Stu didn't think so. Not JoAnna. Not the supremely confident JoAnna. She was glad to be rid of the baby, and she seemed sorry only that in its brief life it had led her to marry Stu. But now she had gotten rid of him, too, and she was back where she started—free and in the driver's seat.

Brody peered at Stu from across the table. "Thinking?" he asked. "Don't think," he raised his index finger, "drink."

The GI pulled JoAnna's head back by the hair and poured beer into her. She was beyond drunk by now, and the GI used her like a doll, seeing what he could make her do. He pulled the bayonet from her chest and offered it to whoever wanted to kill her.

"No?" he said when Stu refused. "No? That's all right. There's lots of killers here."

JoAnna lolled against one and then another, dying at the hands of many men. It seemed out of character—a sign of something deeply wrong—but at the same time, Stu thought, no humiliation could really touch someone like JoAnna. Some of the men lifted her from the floor and ground their hips against her.

Stu's father thought that Stu should fight. The news that his brother was missing had changed his father. He was like somebody who drops a stone down a well but doesn't hear it hit bottom. More than anything else, what he wanted was another stone. "You're lost," he said at dinner one night. "Army would give you someplace to go, something to do."

Stu knew the chances. They'd send him to Vietnam. "I got nothing at all against those people over there," Stu said.

His father's eyebrows pitched steeply together in a V that made him look fierce, like the eagle on a dollar bill, even when he was only confused. "How you know that?" he said. "Your trouble is you don't know who you got something against."

"All you get in that war," Stu said, "is gone. One way or another."

His father shook his head. "Look who's talking. You're gone right now and don't even know it. At least your brother is doing something."

"Yeah? What?"

"Democracy." His father tapped the table with the steak knife. "Equality."

"Yeah," said Stu, "everybody missing is gone just the same amount."

"No," his father said. "Some are more missing than others. At least your brother's missing for his country."

"Kill me," JoAnna said, "before I multiply." She held the bayonet out toward Stu there in the bar. The GI's gun was at the back of her head.

"If you're going to join anything," his mother had said, "what you ought to join is a church."

The knife in his father's hand dipped toward the dinner table. "As if the boy doesn't have enough trouble."

"What church you think I ought to join, Mom?"

"Why . . ." she said. Then her gaze drifted off and she was in God's waiting room again. There was no talking to her about religion. Stu had watched his mother argue with a sidewalk preacher once. The man harangued, but his mother was unmoved. She simply said over and over, "God is big. God is big," as if she had taken the measurements herself. Now, she looked at Stu from far away. "Why," she said, "your own, of course."

"Shit," his father said. "What he better do is figure out who the enemy is."

"Who could it be," his mother said, "other than God?"

"Kill me," JoAnna said. She was so drunk she could hardly stand. "If I multiply, more will die."

The GI dropped his gun and grabbed JoAnna's waist from behind, shoving his hips into her with such force that the record in the juke-box skipped. "Utt oh," people said. The dancers stopped, but the GI kept it up, JoAnna's head bobbing to his rhythm. When the GI stopped, the record went on its way again, and the dancers danced.

The guy pulled JoAnna to his side. "You know more than you're telling," he said. Then he took the blindfold from her eyes and headed her toward the back of the bar, where a door led to the heater room.

Brody leaned across the table. "Man," he said, "this ain't right."

"What's that?"

"This Halloween business with your wife is what."

"I'm not watching," Stu said, "and I don't know nothing. That's why I'm so goddamn happy."

"Well," Brody said, "it ain't no treat." Brody rose from his chair and stepped in front of the GI. "You ain't right," he said. "Who the fuck you think you are?"

The man smiled down at Brody. He unzipped his coveralls to reveal the black uniform and the badge. "I been there," he said. "I done what my country wanted, and now I'm back, and I *am* what's right."

Brody blinked, and the GI stepped around him, disappearing with JoAnna into the back room.

Brody sat down again. "You all right?" he asked Stu.

When you weld, you set the tension on your mask so a little nod of the head is all it takes to bring it down into place. Just a little "yes," and what would have blinded you becomes beautiful. Stu nodded. The brightest parts barely showed, and the rest was shadow. "I'm all right," he said.

In the back room, the VC was groaning, dying. She screamed. She pleaded to be killed. Guys stood around the door worried, trying to help. No.

"Too big," Stu heard himself say.

"Huh?"

"God is too fucking big."

A guy Stu knew at the factory thought welds were so beautiful that it was a shame you had to look at them through dark glass. "I want to see one with the necked eye," he said, and the way he pronounced the word made the welds sound sexy and forbidden. Then he did it. One day he flipped the mask up, put the gun in place, pulled the trigger, and stared for as long as he could stand it. They led him away after that, and for a long time, he was blind. When he recovered, he said there was a worm-shaped spot, dark as night, in the middle of whatever he saw. As bright as that weld had been bright, the spot was dark. "It's a damn shame," he said. "I seen the beauty with my eyes, but it has ruined me for the world."

When the guy in olive drab came out, he smiled: "Don't nobody kill like I do. You want to try? Go ahead," he said. "Try." And one by one some of the guys who had been standing around *did* try.

JoAnna begged. "Kill me," she cried, and they tried. Stu could hear them in there trying.

The cop leaned down and put his hands on their table. "I seen what people get," he said, "and her . . ." he jerked his head toward the back room, "she ain't getting nothing."

"You're a motherfucker," Brody said.

"No," the olive drab said. "She's no mother, and a good thing, too."

Stu stood up. The cop's badge was at eye level. Stu threw up his hand to shade his eyes, and the cop's head jerked back. Stu turned away, still trying to cover his eyes, but everywhere faces turned upward. The door flashed as it swung open. Then there was the night air, and the sky, huge, and the stars burning holes.

In the kudzu, Stu inhaled and held his breath. Time slowed. The less you knew, the better off you were. Car doors closed, engines started. Gravel crunched under tires. It must be the same car leaving again and again without returning—time skipping like a bad record.

He was looking down at his hands as they rolled a joint in the dim green light. They were Vernon's hands, and Vernon's voice was in his ears: "Got it knocked, don't you?" Vernon said. "You don't show. That's how these gooks whip our asses so bad. They don't show, neither."

The door of the bar opened again, and Stu heard her voice. Not the same voice saying things he'd heard before. It was something with time in it. She was sobbing and Brody was walking beside her, helping her stand.

"We don't hate them," she said, "We just don't *want* them, right?"

"What's that?"

"They want what we got."

"Sure," Brody said. "Let's get you home, okay?"

"Where's he?"

"Don't know," Brody said. "He was at my table, but he left."

"He'll turn up."

"Yeah."

"MIA."

"Right."

Stu stepped from the kudzu cave and stood beneath the street light. He could see her now as if he had flipped up a mask. The corners of her eyes had washed away, and the yellow of her face was streaked with her real color. As JoAnna and Brody stumbled toward Brody's car, Stu could see how haggard she was. Not the conquering JoAnna, not the woman he had admired. Better not to know, he told himself, but there she was, sorry and weak enough now to want him again.

"He'll turn up," she said, never looking over to where he stood.

"Yeah," said Brody. Then they got into his car and pulled out.

Brody's taillights faded like the last hot spots in a weld, but what JoAnna had done burned a darkness into Stu, and his only hope now was that he could find a way to live with the blindness it left.

The Grease
Man

S ound bounced around so badly in the warehouse that Stu did not recognize the footsteps. Whoever was down there sounded like he was looking for something but not having much luck. The steps paced and circled, and shoes shuffled on concrete.

Stu laid his hand on his grease gun, just in case. He was way up near the ceiling, where he had made a sort of office for himself out of stuff he'd scrounged from the factory. Stacks of boxes made the walls, and a big plastic bag of Handy Rags served for a chair. An overturned bucket was his table. Swallows swooped among the rafters, and cool breezes stirred up the smell of cardboard. The dozen big loading doors framed scenes of the swamp outside. There were willows along the causeway, foxtails bending in the wind, and stretches of open water ruffled and shimmering. Stoop-shouldered Pressy, the old waterman, waded knee-deep in the water, his boat following behind him by a line tied around his waist.

It was a fine place up there, finer than Stu's father ever had bucking a chainsaw all his life. He was his own boss, his father used to tell Stu, but Stu had discovered that if you worked it right, you could be your own boss at the factory, too. You didn't have to be God of it all. All you had to be was God over your own little part, your own cog.

Out through the big doors, he watched Pressy lift a foot from the water and put it down again toe first, like a ballet dancer. His arms were out from his sides for balance. He stood very still except that he was twisting his toes into the mud. Stu knew what was coming. Pressy backed up a step and bent over. He pushed both hands into the

mud until his face was only inches from the water. Chunks of muck
fell from the thing he brought up. It was a sort of magic, Stu thought,
pulling money from the mud like that.

Now there was only the sound of somebody climbing, picking his
way up among the boxes. Stu raised his gun. He was just about to
take the back way out when Hooks's face, square and black, rose over
the boxes.

Stu grabbed a handful of rags.

Hooks looked at Stu, then at the newspaper and the rag-bag chair.
His nose wrinkled.

"Everything's fine," Stu said. He touched his ear. "I can tell."

Hooks's big, bloodshot eyes blinked slowly. He gave a sort of sideways nod, and motioned for Stu to follow him back down the boxes.

Soon, they stood in the main aisle of the warehouse. Tow-motors
hummed past, and End Men used overhead cranes to move five-ton
rolls of finished linoleum from The Machine.

"Running fine," Stu said.

"Come with me," Hooks said, and he turned and limped toward
the far end of the warehouse where large metal doors led to The
Machine. He opened one and motioned Stu in, but a roar like bull-
dozers and jet liners seemed to hold him back. It was fifty degrees
hotter in there and the air smelled of burned paint.

Hooks shoved him forward.

The Machine was three stories high and as long as a city block.
Paint Zombies paced on their balconies at all three levels. They
tended rollers that applied layers of paint to the endless, moving
sheet of sixteen-foot-wide felt. Their job was to make the colors
even and to keep flying insects from getting into the paint before the
felt got to the ovens.

Lights near the ceiling glowed yellow in the smoky air, and the
Zombies never really seemed awake. At break time, they would stare
right past you. Stu thought they couldn't see things that didn't move.

Hooks bent his head toward Stu. "Don't leave the job no more,"
he shouted. His bottom teeth stuck up—crooked as old tombstones.
"Don't read, don't watch no scenery. Don't do nothing but grease."

Hooks brought his face inches from Stu's. "This thing . . ." He

waved a hand at The Machine. "Got its own mind, and you don't know what it thinks. I slap this motherfucker. I spit on it. I put a bit in its goddamn mouth. I kick the motherfucker. This bitch will do what I tell it to. And so will you."

Stu could not seem to stop smiling. There was nothing to get mad at. It was just a dumb machine. Two miles of felt that would eventually be floor covering snaked around four hundred and fifteen rollers through ovens and around paint rollers and cool rollers. That was 830 grease bearings. He knew the number exactly because it was his job to grease every one of them, and not just grease but to know which ones were starting to chatter, which ones were hotter than they ought to be, which ones were getting ready to scream.

Stu lifted a finger toward his ear. He was going to explain his gift, his special talent—he could hear what others could not, but Hooks grabbed his hand. "What I don't give," he shouted, "is a single green goddamn about what you think." He turned Stu around and pushed him toward his work.

Stu put on his gloves and snapped the nozzle of his gun onto a little tit-shaped grease fitting. He gave a couple pumps and then pulled the nozzle off and went to the next fitting. Hooks watched him for a while. Then he was gone.

Stu snapped and pumped, snapped and pumped. Most of the time the grease just ran out of the fittings because the bearings were already full. Meanwhile, yellow linoleum with red squares rolled by non-stop, over roller and under roller.

Hooks limped around on the catwalks, sometimes up by the ceiling near the Number Three Oven, sometimes down by the Number One Paint Machine. No telling where he'd turn up. Stu fell into daydreams, looking off into the distance that wasn't there. Then all of a sudden, Hooks was beside him, big marbles of sweat on his forehead and his tongue jumping out from behind his teeth like a fat, pink frog. When he shouted, though, it was strange because all Stu heard was The Machine.

A little later, the felt ripped apart as it was screaming through Number Three Oven, way up by the ceiling. The ragged end slapped out over the Cool Roller and sailed thirty feet down to the floor. The

siren sounded, and The Machine stopped. It was a strange quiet then with only the hiss of gas from the ovens. The Cool Roller shined. It was fat as a big tree, and it sat outside Number Three Oven, hissing and spitting and leaking water. When everything was right, a steady stream of hot felt rolled over it, smoking and screaming. But now the roller was bare, and it shined like something that didn't belong where it was.

Hooks put a coil of rope over his shoulder and climbed up on top of the roller, balancing like a lumberjack on a log. He cussed at the men on the floor below and then dropped one end of the rope down to First Level, where the End Men cut the felt into a curve shaped like the end of a finger. They tied one end of the rope to it, and Hooks wrapped the other end around the Cool Roller. He walked the roller like a lumberjack, and slowly, the felt rose off the floor—a finger growing longer and longer until at last it touched Hooks's feet. He grabbed the felt and made a Paint Zombie help him splice it to the other end.

Stu clapped his hands together and flicked his wrist so that his gloves slipped off and lay there with the fingers slightly curled. He was only too happy to stand around at times like this, glad that he did not have to risk his neck to do his job. Still, he worked all day in the hot, screaming noise, and by the time he clocked out, he was beat. It felt good to walk away from the factory, but he could still hear The Machine in his head and he could still smell its smell.

When he got home, JoAnna had burgers ready to cook, and she had opened a bottle of wine and poured some into the custard dishes they used for wine glasses. It had taken two years, but Stu thought JoAnna had finally gotten used to him. He wasn't what she wanted, but she had begun to treat him like a project, and he was willing enough to be worked on.

Stu sat down at the kitchen table and sighed.

"Tired?" she said.

He nodded. He could never tell what went on in her eyes. They were so dark he just fell right in every time—lost in her beauty, in her untouchability.

She smiled. Being tired meant you were working hard, she thought.

And that meant you were getting somewhere. Her idea was that Stu needed to work his way up into the real money at the plant.

"Boss is riding me," Stu admitted. "Had to hump that machine all day."

JoAnna sipped her wine and frowned.

Stu wanted to curl up in those eyes.

"When you rise," she said, "Mr. Factory won't be able to drag you down."

Stu didn't have the heart to tell her how many people would have to die before he could become relief man, much less shift supervisor, much less foreman.

She laid the burgers in the pan and turned toward him. Her hand went to her stomach. She was pregnant again, but Stu was afraid to hope this time. The first one had not survived, though in its brief time, it had made JoAnna need him. That child turned Stu into a hero just by the fact that he was there and willing to marry a girl who had gotten in trouble.

She went off the deep end after the miscarriage, sorry that she had married Stu for nothing, as it turned out. She left him and tried to land the guy she really loved, but it didn't work, and so she had come back. Again, all he had to do was be there. She didn't really come back to Stu, though. She came back to the idea of what she could make Stu into. Now she was pregnant with his kid, and he sensed that just being there was not going to be enough this time.

He went upstairs to take a shower and change. JoAnna had laid out his clothes for the next day—a pair of dark blue pants and a lighter blue work shirt with an oval over the pocket that said "Jakes." She thought looking successful meant you were going to *be* successful.

Stu stood in the shower and let the water hit his back. He thought about Hooks losing one piece of himself after the other to The Machine. For thirty years, another tooth gone, another finger missing, a crushed foot, a twisted spine. After thirty years of that, Hooks was an angry man shaking his fist at a machine. No, Stu was not taking that way up. Every piece of The Machine had to run just right for the whole thing to work. If just one thing was wrong, nothing else mattered. There was power in that. Every little cog, every little pin,

was its own sort of god. The world was big, God was big, but if you knew how to work one little part, you could make a space for yourself. When he went down for dinner, he smiled and slapped JoAnna on the rear end.

She spun around and backed up against the kitchen counter. "What's got you frisky?"

He smiled. It was all going to be fine. They sat down to dinner, and Stu ate his burger, happy and confident.

The next day, he moved his office out of the warehouse. He took JoAnna's picture off the rafter it was taped to and picked up the rest of yesterday's newspaper that he never had a chance to finish.

His new office was in the Paint Room just off the Number Two Paint Machine. Half a dozen tanks twenty feet tall filled up most of the place, and there were so many pipes and hoses worming around that you could hardly see from one end of the room to the other. A catwalk went along the tops of the tanks so Paint Men could pour in pigment and thinner and whatnot. The whole place smelled like solvent, and it made Stu a little dizzy at first.

Back under the eaves behind a stack of pigment drums was a greasy little window and a small piece of open floor. Stu squeezed in and taped JoAnna's picture to the wall. He dusted off a place to sit and snapped open the paper. It wasn't as nice as the warehouse, but it was a whole lot more private.

He finished the paper and sat for a while looking out the window. The swamp was not so pretty from this angle. Paint Men spilled pigment over the years, so the ground was red and black, and the water shined in the sun like a rainbow. Some of the weeds were dead, and patches of red drifted into the swamp.

Pressy was there, though, poling his boat just beyond the red water, stepping into the mud from time to time to hunt loggerhead turtles. When Stu was still in junior high, Pressy caught one that had two heads. He put it in a tub in his backyard and charged a dime for kids to see. It was real popular with Stu's friends even though one of the heads wasn't really a full head at all—it was just a head-shaped bump that didn't have any eyes or a mouth. Pressy said he caught it in the red water out by the factory.

It was ten o' clock before Stu slipped out of the Paint Room and started greasing. He had waited so long that The Machine was running rough. Some of the bearings grumbled, and a few were hot enough to melt their grease and drip little pools of brown on the metal floor. Stu snapped the nozzle onto the nipples and pumped a couple loads into each bearing until, one-by-one, they quieted down.

After an hour, he was up by the Cool Roller, the heaviest one in The Machine because of all the water it held. Stu put half a load of grease into its bearings and then listened closely. They grumbled, but not too badly. Then he touched the bearing caps. They were hot, but not too hot.

He went back to his office, but he didn't have to wait long before the siren went off. The Machine stopped, and Stu heard Hooks cussing orders. The siren went off three more times before lunch. It was just a little thing—a short-greased Cool Roller, but it made a difference like God. Stu opened the window just enough to let in a little fresh air, but it didn't mix too well with the solvent smell.

After lunch, Stu heard clanking on the catwalk. Hooks limped closer and closer, hollering for Stu. When his paint-spotted boot slid into the Stu's office, Stu flattened himself against the wall and tried to come up with some excuse for being there. But Hooks was too fat to squeeze through the opening, and when the siren went off again, he limped away muttering.

Stu sighed. Hooks's numbers would suffer because of one short-greased roller. There would be shake-ups. There would be opportunities.

On the way home from work, he stopped by Pressy's and got two dozen blue crabs.

"For what?" JoAnna said.

"Celebration." Stu smiled, but the solvent fumes had given him a headache. One minute he felt fine and the next he didn't.

JoAnna put away the spaghetti she had been ready to make. "For?"

"Possibilities."

"What possibilities?" JoAnna said.

"Whatever I want," he said.

JoAnna looked at the crabs.

"Drop them in the spaghetti water," Stu told her.

"Still moving?"

"That's how you do it."

JoAnna shook her head and backed away, so Stu dumped the crabs in. They were silent when they hit the boiling water, but JoAnna's hand went to her mouth, and she turned away.

"Shut it off in five minutes," he told her. "I'm going to change."

He took a shower, and when he went down for dinner, JoAnna had the pot of crabs on the table.

Stu snapped off a claw and broke it in half. He pulled out the pink meat with his teeth and slid it into his mouth on the tip of his tongue. He chewed and smiled.

"You just *look* like a man who knows what he's doing," JoAnna said. "Born to make something of yourself, Stuart Jakes." She slid crab meat into her mouth and chewed. "Mmm," she said. "They may not *look* good, but they *are* good."

It was funny how the headaches from the paint fumes came and went with no warning.

The next day Stu clocked in early so he wouldn't run into Hooks. Night shift greased The Machine in the regular way, so he wouldn't have to do anything for a few of hours. He made his way to his office, and as soon as he was back in the paint smell, his headache seemed to disappear.

Mid-morning, he put on his gloves and headed out. He was just about to snap onto the grease fitting of the Cool Roller when the siren went off. The Machine stopped, and the ragged end of felt slapped out of the oven next to him and sailed slow-motion style down to the floor. Everything was quiet then except for the hiss of gas from the ovens.

Hooks's voice was in Stu's ear. "Where you been, Grease?"

"Working. Machine's running bad." Stu tapped his ear. "I'm steady greasing."

Hooks grabbed Stu by the arm and made him get up on the Cool Roller. The End Men had already cut the felt into a curve and tied the rope to it. Hooks told Stu to walk the roller.

Pulling thirty feet of felt close up was hard work even when the roller wasn't dragging. Stu tried to look like he was not straining too much. The felt rose, a finger pointing straight up at Stu. Finally, the tip curved around the roller, and Hooks yelled for him to stop. He went to the control panel and tapped the temperature gauge. Hook's tongue slipped out from behind his teeth, and he nodded.

"All right," he said. "A hundred and thirty degrees. Come on, Jakes. You're the one who thinks he knows this son of a bitch machine so good."

End Men and Paint Zombies gathered around to watch because making a splice inside the oven was the most dangerous job in the whole factory. The Zombies nodded their heads and looked at Stu like they were wise. Nobody smiled.

Hooks handed Stu a roll of eight-inch tape. He slapped Stu on the back and shoved him forward. Stu stood at the mouth looking in. The oven was a hundred feet long and twenty feet wide. It was open on each end, and the felt went through it on rollers. It was only four feet high inside, though, and there wasn't really enough room for a man to get around in. The air temperature was down to a hundred and thirty, but the metal floor and ceiling were still three hundred and fifty.

"Hooks," Stu said, "I got this headache."

"Shut up."

Stu bent down and stepped inside. His chest got big when he inhaled, but it didn't feel as if any air was going in. He and Hooks grabbed the felt and pulled it deeper into the oven. They had to work bent over, and if they pulled too hard and fell on that hot floor, why somebody was going to have to scrape them up with a spatula. Soon the bottoms of Stu's boots were too hot for comfort. Then, without any warning, Hooks dropped his side of the felt. Stu was pulling so hard that he lost his balance and had to catch himself with one hand. It only took a couple seconds to burn through the glove and sear his skin.

Hooks watched. The sweat that dropped from his face turned to steam when it hit the floor. Stu could see the blue from the pilot lights shining in Hooks' eyes. "You ain't been doing your job, Jakes." Hooks tongue pushed his top lip out. "I ought to leave you in here to cook."

Stu shook his burned hand, but the air was so hot that it only burned more.

Hooks lapped the two ends of felt over each other and made a straight cut through both layers. Then he grabbed the roll of tape from Stu and peeled off a start. "Hold the roll," he said.

Stu didn't grab it right away because his hand hurt.

"Hold the roll," Hooks said, "or we'll stay in here until we die."

Stu put one hand into each end of the roll, and Hooks yanked. The tape screamed coming off. Four big screams. Then quiet. Then four more screams, and the splice was done.

"Go!" Hooks said. "Go!"

He moved fast through the oven, sideways, like a crab, and Stu was on his heels. His shoes were burning, and his hand was killing him. There was no air, only heat. Stu was so dizzy he thought he was going to pass out right there in the oven, pass out and burn to death. But then he thought about JoAnna and about the baby, and he found a way to keep going.

End Men squinted into the oven. Their faces wavered in the heat.

Stu could see what was going to happen. He knew The Machine so well that it told him the future: Hooks would beat him out of the oven by ten feet. He would jump onto the Cool Roller, which he would expect to move freely, but it wouldn't because it was not greased right. Probably, Hooks would lose his balance. Probably he would fall backwards into the oven. It was a gift of vision given to a cog-god like Stu. But it didn't help him know what he should do. He could shout for Hooks to watch out, but then the man would know that Stu had been messing up and that would be the end of his job. Where would JoAnna and he be then?

Everything was sweat and tiredness and confusion. Stu was going to pass out and burn to death right there in the oven. He was dizzy, and sweat was in his eyes. His ears buzzed, and he got a picture in his head that didn't make sense, like in a dream, of that two-headed turtle that only had one real head.

Hooks stopped for a second and looked back. He was soaked with sweat.

Stu wanted to say something, but he thought about JoAnna and the baby and didn't know what to do.

Hooks grinned his tombstone smile. Then he turned and jumped for the roller. He did a little shuffle step on top, his arms out from his sides for balance. Then his hands started making circles. His foot slipped, and at first Stu couldn't really tell he was falling, it started so slowly. Hooks leaned back farther and farther until his feet slid down the side of the roller, and he landed on his back in the oven. His shirt started to smoke the moment he hit.

Stu didn't know how he managed, but he was suddenly there, pulling Hooks up. Some of the skin from the man's back stayed on the floor, though, smoking and stinking. Two End Men took Hooks by the arms and half-walked and half-carried him out of the oven. They all stopped on the catwalk, and Hooks looked at Stu. He was in pain, and he didn't understand.

The End Men carried him off.

"You sure moved fast in there at the last," said a Zombie.

"Only way to do," Stu said, "when you're in hell."

He went back to his office and stared out the window for a while. Pressy was nowhere to be seen, and the red water seemed to be spreading through the swamp. He peeled JoAnna's picture off the wall and headed back to lay a big load of grease in the Cool Roller.

Then he found another office way down inside The Machine, back behind the Number One Paint Roller. It stank, and it was hot. The noise was so loud that Stu could not hear a thing. He was hidden so deep inside The Machine that nobody would ever find him now. The new foreman, whoever he might be, might not really believe there is a Grease Man.

Stu slid the glove gingerly off his hand. He squeezed grease from his gun and painted it over the burns. His glove lay before him, the fingers curled in an empty grip. Stu tried to stick JoAnna's picture up on the side of The Machine, but everything in there shook so badly that it wouldn't stay up more than a couple seconds at a time.

Salvage

The two huge Dobermans, Death and Plunder, were on them before the sheet-metal gate in the junkyard's fence could even bang back into place. They knew Stu, and usually they gave his steel-toed boots plenty of room, but Gloria was new to them, and so they closed in on her with their teeth bared and their tails in the air. Stu bent down. "It's all right," he said as he picked his daughter up. "They're not brave."

Gloria's fingers dug into the flesh at the back of his neck, and she began to cry. Each step the animals took raised her pitch until it felt to Stu as if he was holding an air-raid siren on his hip.

Death was just a step away when Stu made his move. The kick landed in the dog's ribs, but Death just grunted and stood there snarling. Plunder circled, looking for the easy opening. Stu swung his lunch box and almost caught him in the jaw. The dogs conferred. Ears rose. Death's tongue unrolled from his head in a long yawn, and Plunder nosed up some scent, which he followed in a winding way up the hill that was parked thick with wrecks and junkers. Tier after tier rose from the river, their broken windshields and dead lights keeping a blind watch on the water below.

Plunder disappeared into the wrecks, and Death cast a glance over his shoulder at Stu. Then he too was gone—up the hill and into the foreign cars.

Stu tried to put Gloria down, but she wrapped both arms around his. When he managed to peel her off, she wrapped herself around his leg. It was like trying to let go of a caterpillar. He popped her on the head with his palm and shook her loose from his leg. "Don't!" he said.

Gloria stood there staring at him—silent. Wordlessness surrounded her like a shell. She took everything in—that was clear to anyone who watched her—but she gave nothing back. In her four years, she had never spoken a word. The girl had her mother's bottomless brown eyes, and Stu had come to believe that she had inherited her mother's resentment of him as well.

He took her hand, and they walked up the hillside, rising through the foreign cars and into the Chevrolets, where Stu stopped and looked back down the hill. Only the roofs and windows of wrecks showed above the weeds, and beyond them was the river where mist hung above the water.

Gloria raised her arms.

"Ask," Stu said, but she only put a fist to her mouth and stared at the ground.

The neighbor woman who usually took care of Gloria was dying of cancer. She had called that morning before sunrise to say she just couldn't work any longer. Stu and JoAnna had known this was coming. They had tried to prepare for it, but they had not found anyone else they could afford. JoAnna worked in a cotton mill, and Stu was a parts worm at the yard. Between them, they earned enough to make payments on their debts and to buy the necessities, but they didn't even have a car since the Valiant had died, and neither one could afford to miss work. There was no way JoAnna could take the girl into the mill, so Stu was stuck with her.

"Want me to carry you?" he said.

Gloria smiled.

"All you've got to do is ask."

The girl hunched her shoulders and rolled her knuckles over her lips.

When the pregnancy that made them get married in the first place ended at five months, they should have taken it as a sign. But back then, all JoAnna wanted was to get pregnant again. And she did. It was a make-up pregnancy, and before Gloria was a year old JoAnna saw how she had tricked herself. For a while, she tried to help Stu be what she hoped he could become. But when Stu got a job working for Pressy, JoAnna was not happy. It was a shapeless, do everything sort of job, and worse yet, much of it involved a junk yard. No, it was not what she had envisioned. Her list of Stu's failings shrank to only one item—he was Stu. Their daughter's bottomless brown eyes and endless silences seemed to echo that verdict.

Stu held Gloria's hand, and they made their way up through the Fords and Oldsmobiles, and when they got to the Chryslers, Stu put his hands on Gloria's shoulders and stopped her near a wrecked New Yorker.

"Look," he said.

But Gloria would not.

He pushed her closer. The front end of the car was a twisted mess of metal and weeds. The driver's door was gone, and two starbursts in the windshield showed where people's heads must have hit the glass. Stu put his hand under Gloria's chin and forced her to look at the wreck. The driver's seat and the floors were stained black from what Stu supposed was blood. He wanted to pry his daughter's mind open and release the words he was sure were in there. He wanted to hear her tell him just where and how he was wrong.

Gloria tried to turn away from the wreck, but Stu would not let her. She squirmed and grunted. "Talk," he said. "What's wrong?"

Gloria stopped. Her gaze fastened on something in the car. Stu looked up and saw, leaning from the dashboard, one of those old plastic figurines on a magnetic base. He could never tell for sure who these things were supposed to be with their flowing robes and their outstretched arms. Saints, he supposed, or Jesus.

"Want that?"

Gloria's eyes widened. JoAnna used to buy dolls for the girl, but Gloria preferred toy cars. When she got a doll, she'd push it along the floor, car-style, for a while, but before long she'd go back to her other toys. A few days later, they'd find the doll buried somewhere in the yard. JoAnna said it gave her the shivers. Stu reached into the wreck and pulled the figure from the dash. He handed it to Gloria. "Listen real good," he said, "and tell me what he says."

Gloria clutched the figure by the middle, and Stu turned them away from the wreck. They continued upward, through the Mercurys and Buicks. Stu stopped now and then to get more stuff—Playboy bunny heads, dangly dice, pine-tree air fresheners, more figurines. He carried a handful past the Lincolns and Cadillacs and into the high corner of the yard reserved for pickup trucks.

The El Camino shined there like a vision in the morning sun. Half car, half truck, it was graceful as a sculpture and white as goodness. Hardly a dent in it. Chrome wheels, dual exhausts, driving lights, fancy antennas. Somebody spent a lot of time on that truck, and Stu thought it was a shame to find it in the yard. Wouldn't take much, he was convinced, to get it going again.

He dumped the knickknacks into the bed of the El Camino. Then he lifted Gloria over the tailgate and sat her down in the midst of the stuff. She hardly noticed the toys, though. She just stared at her father, and the old unspoken blame seemed to close in on him again. He pulled away from her and climbed into the El Camino's cab.

Coffee from his thermos warmed his mind. He watched the junk-yard below—terrace after terrace of cars stepping down the hillside toward the misty river. He sipped coffee and slipped into his favorite daydream: The El Camino running smooth and strong and him driv-ing that graceful white blur down the highway with his daughter in the seat next to him, singing. In the daydream her head was turned toward the open window, though, so the wind pulled her words away and he could never hear what she said.

He was not even finished with that first cup when he heard Pressy rattle the lock on the tool shed door. Stu slid out of the cab and leaned into the bed of the truck. He meant to tell Gloria to be quiet, but then he shook his head. What was he thinking?

At the shed, Pressy leaned against a post. He was wearing his usual greasy clothes and dilapidated boots. His hands were lined with per-manent dirt, and his blue eyes burned like acetylene in his dark face. Standing next to him was that bowlegged Doberman, Death. The dog lowered his head and looked balefully at Stu.

"W'hell," Pressy said, "Stu."

Death circled, scenting.

"Ready to turn the wish-they-was-living into the glad-they's-dead?" Pressy said.

Stu's job as parts worm was to take usable things off old cars. When he was done, only hulks remained, empty shells with dangling tubes and unbolted shafts. It was depressing work, and if it hadn't been for the El Camino, it would have gotten him down. But the truck was a kind of healing.

They began their ritual walk around the yard. Pressy pointed at cars they passed and told Stu what parts to take from which. They were among Buicks when the Gloria-siren started. Somehow it was different from its previous wail. Death should have been howling along with the noise, his head thrown back against the sky. But Death was nowhere to be seen.

"I want the guts out of this," Pressy was saying, meaning that Stu was to take the engine and transmission from the Century. But Stu had already turned away and was breasting through the weeds toward the El Camino.

"Hey," Pressy said, and Stu could hear the weeds slapping Pressy's shoes as he followed. "Dammit," Pressy said, "what's wrong with you?"

When they got to the pickups, Death was already there trying to climb his bowlegged way into the back of the El Camino. His front feet were clawed over the top of the tailgate, and one back foot pawed for a step on the bumper. Gloria had backed herself against the cab. Her mouth was a small, dark circle, but the sound coming from it was pitched to crack the girl in pieces.

Stu kicked the dog's only planted leg out from under him, and Death clung to the tailgate for a second before he fell. Stu snatched Gloria from the truck and covered her mouth with the palm of his hand. The dog was up in a second. He bared his teeth and began to move in, but Pressy grabbed his collar.

"Don't," he said, turning toward Stu, "ever kick my dog."

Stu and Pressy stared at each other.

"Look," Stu said, "this here's my daughter. I had to bring her to work because her babysitter is dying."

Pressy reached into the weeds with his free hand and pulled out an old tire. He sat it upright and slapped it down the hill. "Go git it!" he said to Death, and the dog headed out. "Good boy," Pressy shouted, "now, tear it up!"

Sounds of the struggle between Death and the tire drifted up the hill. "It's a good dog I got there," Pressy said, "and I don't need you to cripple him."

Stu took his hand from his daughter's mouth. She was quiet. He tried to sit her in the midst of her toys again, but she would not let go of his sleeve. "What was I supposed to do?" Stu said. "Let your dog eat my daughter?"

"This ain't kindergarten."

After his skirmish with the tire, Death, tongue dangling, climbed slowly up the hill and stood next to Pressy, who nudged the dog with his knee and nodded toward Stu. "Ever seen such a mess of a man?"

The dog gathered up his tongue and stared.

"Just let her stay today is all," Stu said. "I've got no place to take her." He tried to peel Gloria's hands from his shirt. "Let me part out something nearby. That way I can keep an eye on her."

Pressy rested a hand on the El Camino and looked at Gloria.

She was silent. Her gaze was blank.

"What's wrong with her?" he said.

"Nothing's wrong with her."

Pressy shook his head and swept his hand in a gesture that took in the entire yard. "Something," he said, "is wrong with everything. Don't take a genius to figure that out."

"Well, I ain't no genius," Stu said, "but there is nothing wrong with this girl."

Pressy smiled. There were gaps between his teeth. "You're like people that drive old, beat-up cars I see on the road, ain't you, Jakes? Junk that they don't know is junk. I want to go up to people like that and tell them that I got just the place for what they're driving. But I don't do it, and you know why? Because I feel sorry for people like that. That's why." Pressy narrowed his eyes. "You stay right here today and pull the guts out of this." He patted the El Camino. "But no kids no more after this."

Stu stepped back and put his hand on the truck's roof. "You want the guts out of this?"

"Mmm-hmm."

"But it's a driver."

Wrinkles made rays around Pressy's eyes. "Jakes," he said. "Either something *is* junk or it is going to *be* junk. I got that figured out early in my life, and it made me rich."

"Look," Stu said, "the engine's clean, it's not been hit. Bound to be some squirrelly little thing wrong is all."

Pressy nudged Death again. "Nothing wrong with this truck and nothing wrong with his empty-eyed daughter, neither."

Death panted a grin.

"Every parts worm I ever hired figured he was going to fix this or that and drive out of here in some kind of style," Pressy said. "Nobody ever done it, though, and you want to know how come, Jakes? Because y'all ain't good for nothing but tearing stuff up is how come."

Stu looked out across the yard. It was going to be hot. The mist had risen from the river, and the water looked as red and thick as transmission fluid. Already, the air was oily with the smell of wrecks, and the cicadas had started their crazy chant. Stu's mind filled with the buzz of the junkyard's bugs.

Pressy pulled another tire from the weeds and slapped it down the hill. "Git it!" he told the dog.

Death looked sideways at him and then walked slowly down the hill. Pressy disappeared into the weeds after the dog. "Tear it up!" Stu heard him holler. "Goddamn you, I said tear it up!"

For weeks, Stu had worked on the El Camino, stealing twenty minutes here and there to replace battery, ballast resistor, solenoid. But now he had to tear it to pieces, and it was his daughter's fault. He would have liked to know why something that was supposed to be a part of you, something like a kid, could work against you. "See?" he wanted to scream into her face, "See what you've done now?"

He leaned against the El Camino and looked down at Gloria. "It was a way out," was all he said.

The girl sat in the bed of the truck and pushed a figurine around as if its outstretched hands were the front wheels of a car and the circular base under its feet were the rear. She gave it no engine sounds, though, so there was only the unsettling screech of plastic against metal.

"If you're going to use it like a damn car," Stu said, "at least give it some sounds." He reached over the side of the truck and grabbed the figurine. Pushing it car-style, he went, "Voom. See? Voom! Voom!"

He handed it back to her. She put it down car-style but would not even make it move now. Stu shook his head. He turned from the bed of the truck and slid behind the steering wheel.

When he turned the key the radio came on, but the engine would not turn over. Probably it was the starter.

"What's a man supposed to do?" he said to the windshield. His chest tightened. Metallic screeches came from the back of the truck. Stu jumped from the cab and slammed the door. The sound startled the cicadas, and for a second they fell silent. Only a kind of ringing, the sound of crickets, was left in the air.

"Goddamn it, Gloria," Stu said. "Here." He grabbed the figurine. "They're not cars. What you do is make 'em talk, see? That's how you play with dolls. Make 'em say something. It ain't hard. Something like, well, let me see here, 'Hey, you bunnies . . .'"

Stu picked up a Playboy head in the other hand and held it facing the figurine.

"'You bunnies ain't living right? Why don't y'all straig-hten up?'

"And then this other bunny here says, 'Well, Saint Jesus, if you care so much about how she's doing, how come you don't take her out and show her a good time?'

"And then Saint Jesus says, 'All right. Let's head on over to my church . . .'

"See, we'll make a church out of these dice here, and we'll put some pine trees out front. Now, there you go. 'Plus,' says Saint Jesus, 'I got a friend over at the church for you, too.'

"So then the two bunnies are at the church with the two Saint Jesuses, see? Now you take it from there, okay?" Gloria looked up at him, but Stu didn't stay to meet the silence.

Underneath the truck, in the cool, oily dirt, he calmed into his work. He removed the old starter and installed the one he had scavenged from a wreck. The bolts sighed with each turn of the wrench, and there was a simple rightness when they snugged down. He connected the wires and lay there for a minute admiring the job. If he got it running before the day was over, he could still buy it for the salvage price of fifty dollars. He slid out and got behind the wheel, but when he clicked the key to start, nothing happened. He kept the key laid over for a long time while he looked out at the river. Already, the morning's freshness had worn away, and the cicadas had moved onto their weary, ragged, midday buzz.

Stu let go of the key and adjusted the rearview mirror.

Gloria was crashing one Jesus-car into another, soundlessly. He stuck his head out the window. "Look," he said, "I told you not to do that."

Gloria let go of the figurines and scooted herself to the back of the bed.

"Voom!" Stu said. "Say it!"

But she wouldn't.

Stu slapped the side of the truck. The noise shut the cicadas up for another moment, but Gloria hardly flinched. Her eyes went empty of everything but blame. He was not, Stu was not, he could see, good enough.

He pulled his head back inside the cab and sat there with his hands on the wheel. Nothing was in front of him, just weeds and wrecks and a muddy river. He wanted to drive down the ruts in the yard until he came to the gate. Fifty dollars promised to Pressy from next week's pay, and the gate would open to the gravel road. The gravel would lead to blacktop in half a mile, and blacktop, well, blacktop was the world. But it was hard for him to think of the ruts as pathways that led anywhere. They were not roads, or lanes, or even alleys. They were more like the tracks a dead man's heels made when his body was dragged to its final dumping spot.

Stu turned himself upside down in the driver's seat so his head was under the dashboard. Slowly, his eyes adjusted to the dimness. He was just setting to work again when the gloom darkened. Stu tucked his chin toward his chest and looked up.

There stood Pressy, one arm on the El Camino's roof and the other draped over the top of the open door. He was like some dark bird, its wings half extended, its head bobbing downward.

"You two sure make a sight," he said. "Daddy upside down, and the child sitting there like a dumb animal. Don't she play with them things she's got?"

"She plays."

"Yeah? What's she play?"

"Never mind," Stu said.

Pressy walked around the truck. "You ain't done nothing, Jakes. Maybe babysitting and part-worming at the same time ain't going to work out. I got people asking me for jobs every day."

"I'm pulling the dash," Stu lied.

"Well," said Pressy, "dashboards is hell. All that mess of wires that don't nobody know what goes where. Blood in your head, shit in your eyes. Better you than me, Jakes. That's what I say. The thing ain't none of y'all parts worms figured out is my secret."

"Yeah?" said Stu. "What you want from this dash?"

"Gauges, radio."

"Switches?" Stu said. "Fuse box? Flashers?"

"Shit," Pressy said. "Ain't worth dirt. That's just what I'm saying. You ain't learned to give up."

"Got to keep at it," Stu said.

Pressy snorted. "Myself, I got rich by giving up! That's the simplest truth. Giving up. This girl of yours don't know the difference between a person and a car, does she?"

"Gloria," said Stu, "you play right with those things."

"Don't she talk?" Pressy said. "How old is she, anyhow?"

"She'll talk when she's ready to talk."

"Sure she will," said Pressy. "Sure she will. You know, I used to grow corn out here where this yard is. Never had a knack for corn, but I kept at it. I had just got married, and my wife figured I was going to be a big, successful farmer on all this hilly land."

Stu used a screwdriver to pry the sheathing off the steering column so he could get to the ignition switch, which he was sure was the problem. He pulled down on the handle, and the plastic cracked apart loudly.

"Oh yeah!" Pressy said when he heard the noise. "Tear it *up!* You know, the spring after I got married, I figured I'd get a early start farming. It was wet, but that didn't stop me. Only one thing stopped me, and that was when I got my tractor stuck in the mud."

A shower of grit rained down on Stu's face and got into his eyes. He couldn't seem to clear it out because he was upside down.

"Stuck in mud up to its axle," Pressy said. "So I just walked home, picked up the newspaper, and set down next to the stove. You know what my wife said to me?"

Stu dug at his eyes until he saw sparks.

"Jakes? Said you know what she said to me?"

"Huh?"

"She said, 'Ain't you going to *do* something?'"

"'Do something?' I said. 'Nothing but time and dry weather going to get that tractor out.'"

Stu tried to turn onto his side, but his head lodged between the heater and the accelerator pedal, and his legs jammed between the wheel and the seat.

"Now, that's more like it," Pressy said. "At least this girl's playing like Jesus ain't a car. Stabbing him with bunny ears, looks like to me. She got something against Jesus?"

"Ugh," was all Stu could say.

"Anyhow, my wife wouldn't let it alone," Pressy said. "Couldn't I do this? Couldn't I do that? Finally I laid the paper down, and I said, 'Fine.' I took my pickup truck into the field and tried to pull the tractor out. But you know what happened, don't you? Sure you do. Got that truck stuck, too. Walked back to the house and picked up the paper again.

"You listen to me, boy," Pressy said. "My wife acted like it was *my* fault. It was her idea, but it was *my* fault."

"Nuh," Stu said.

Stu rolled onto his back. The pain in his eyes subsided, but tears puddled and he couldn't see.

"I tried to read the paper and let it rain," Pressy said, "but she wouldn't leave that tractor in the field. No sir. Kept it in the kitchen when she cooked, and brought it to dinner when we ate. Had it in front of the TV after that and even took it to bed, too.

"So finally I said, 'All right.' And the next day I took that Oldsmobile she used to drive, and I tried to pull my truck out with it. But you know what happened, don't you? Mmm-hmm. Walked on home again.

"It got so I was eating tractor and sleeping tractor. Felt like I was married to a tractor. Finally, I said to that woman, 'You leave this whole subject alone, now, because I *meant* to put all them vehicles in the mud.'

"'You may be a fool,' she said to me. 'But you ain't that much of a fool.'"

Stu pulled the plastic sheathing off, and the chrome ignition switch shined amid the wires and shafts of the steering column.

"Uh-oh," said Pressy. "Jesuses overboard. They's walking the plank, Jakes. Looks like Playboy is taking over. Gonna be nothing left but rabbits and pine trees. That's life, huh?

"Anyhow, my wife said I was a fool, so I got up from the kitchen table, folded my paper, and put on my hat. I said, 'A fool is blind, woman, and you can't see.'

"I got a ride to the other side of town and bought the ugliest driver I could find at Hurley's Salvage. Cost me thirty-five dollars. Drove it back into this field and parked it next to my wife's Oldsmobile. Then I painted up a sign on plywood—said, 'Car Parts,' and I put it up by the highway.

"First thing I sold was the bumper and the hood off that Oldsmobile. I took the money and bought another junker. My wife was calling me a lot of things then, but fool wasn't one.

"I finally did get that tractor out of the mud. Sure I did—one piece at a time. Most of that first batch is gone now, except for a stray part or two laying in the dirt, but they was like seeds. Got a whole hillside of cars now. Had to build a fence to keep people from stealing. Never had to do that when I was growing corn. I figure you know you got something worth having when somebody wants to steal it."

Stu unbolted the ignition switch and pulled off the electrical connectors. He knew already that there wasn't another one like it in the yard. He wasn'ts sure how to hot wire a car, and he was afraid of ruining something if he connected the wrong wires. No, the best thing would be to fix that switch. It was a chrome cylinder the size of a roll of quarters. He held it in the light and turned it over in his hand, searching for a way in. Only the keyhole offered a glimpse inside, but Stu knew there must be another way.

"Well," Pressy said, "my wife didn't think there was no such thing as a big, successful junkyard owner, so she left, and I sure didn't put no fence around her. She's gone, and I'm rich. All from giving up. See what I'm saying?"

Stu lifted his head and looked up from the floorboard. "Huh?" he said.

"Huh, hell!" Pressy said. "I'm telling you I got rich by quitting. That's the simple truth."

Stu shook his head. "Got to keep at it," he said.

"Your child, Jakes, is beating Jesus to death with dice. It's one thing my wife taught me," Pressy said, "and that is you can't fix people."

"Like I told you," Stu said. "I'm not the giving-up kind."

Pressy backed out of the doorway. "No," he said, "you're probably more like the failing kind."

At noon, Pressy left to eat his lunch. Stu lifted Gloria from the truck and put her on the ground in the shade of the El Camino. He opened a can of peaches and gave Gloria a spoon. Then he spread some toys around. "Don't you crash or stab a thing," he said.

Back in the truck, he chewed his sandwich and stared at the switch. It shined there on the top of the dashboard, nubs and ridges disappearing into the darkness of the keyhole. In his dream, the key clicked over, and the engine churned until it caught. It was a little noisy at first, but Stu revved it, and the valves settled. He drove out of the yard with Gloria sitting next to him. It was not clear where they were headed, but in his dream, the road was long enough to make him think that the world led somewhere.

Gloria banged the can with her spoon, and Stu pulled his mind from the switch. He slid out of the cab. The girl's shirtfront was sticky with peach juice, and Stu used a rag to clean her up. Dirt stuck to her spoon, and it seemed to Stu that some figurines were missing. "Did you bury something?" he said.

Gloria looked up at him, silent.

"Did you?" he said.

She said nothing.

"Burying dolls," he said. "It's not right." His fist grew hard, and he brought it down into the palm of his other hand. Gloria flinched at the sound.

He turned from her and took the chrome switch from the dashboard. It was one of those things that had been put together in a way that was meant to keep you from taking it apart again. Stu could not understand why they made things like this. The plate at the opposite end from the keyhole was crimped to the body of the switch. Stu pried at it with a screwdriver, but he could not loosen it. He tried twisting the plate off with a pair of pliers, but they slipped and pinched his palm. Pain brought a string of curses from him. It made no sense. What was put together in the first place ought to be able to be taken apart in the second. He put the switch on a rock and placed the blade of the screwdriver into a gap in the casing. When his hammer hit the screwdriver, the switch leapt from the rock and zinged into the soft flesh under his chin.

"Jesus Christ!" he said. He held his throat, feeling about to choke on his own Adam's apple. The switch glinted up at him from the weeds where it had fallen. He put it on the rock again, and let his anger take over. The hammer rose and fell. If something made no sense, well then what you did to it shouldn't have to make sense either. It was a relief to hit what resisted him. Finally, the chrome casing cracked and revealed the switch's delicate insides.

He looked up, panting. "Sometimes," he said to Gloria, "that's what it takes."

He picked up the pieces of the switch and studied them. There were deeper secrets yet—other encasements inside the chrome one. His chest tightened. Wires led into plastic boxes, but what happened in there, he had no idea. Breaking them open, he sensed, would destroy them. He looked at Gloria. If something was going to go wrong, whoever made it ought to make a way to fix it, but all he could do was clean off some electrical contacts and stick the thing back together with tape. It felt feeble.

He bolted the switch back in place and connected the wires. Then he slid behind the wheel and put his hand on the key. Gloria stood there on the other side of the truck, framed by the doorway. She had one hand on a figurine's head and the other on its body as if she were ready to screw the lid off a jar.

It wasn't going to work. He knew that. He had only gone through some motions as if mere desire might be enough, as if some force was out there to take pity on him for trying.

The key clicked, but the only other sound the El Camino made was a sickly sort of crackling that came from deep beneath the dash. Smoke drifted into the cab. Gloria backed away.

Stu switched the key to off, but the noise continued and the smoke built. He jumped from the cab and disconnected a battery cable. When the smoke cleared, he bent down and peered under the dash. Where there had been a spaghetti of multicolored wires, there was now only a mass of black and evil-smelling insulation. He straightened up and backed away. The smell in the cab was sickening. He circled to the passenger side.

Gloria backed farther away.

Stu looked down at her, his fists simple as hammers.

"What's wrong?" he said.

Gloria lowered her head.

"Do you want me to hit you?"

She looked up, her eyes bottomless blame.

Stu gritted his teeth. "Do you want me to?" He leaned down until his face was inches from hers. "Say 'No,'" he told her.

She said nothing.

Stu pulled his hand back.

Gloria squeezed her eyes shut.

Stu leaned his back against the ruined truck. He lowered his hand and gazed out over the yard.

Wrecks lined the hillside like a jam of cars trying to cross the river where there was no bridge. They had waited so long that trees had grown into their engines. Instead of crossing, they had given up piece after piece until the world had closed around them and they had settled into the repose of junk.

Stu would give up on the El Camino. He'd let blame settle on his shoulders. He would tear cars apart forever, reduce them to nothing forever. The sun was getting red, and the cicadas had begun the search for their evening rhythm.

Gloria pushed the Jesus-car through some weeds and into the ruts.

Stu sighed. "Voom," he said.

Gloria smiled—it was the timid sort of smile people try when they hope a storm has passed. She pushed the figurine car-style toward her father. Its plastic hands made furrows in the earth. She looked up at him. Her mouth moved. She was silent as a fish at first. The word she managed to say sounded more like "doom" than "voom." But it brightened Stu's heart anyway.

Still Life

His mother's rented hospital bed, huge as an altar, filled the living room, but the woman herself had gotten smaller in the last month: her head more like a skull, her hands all bone and skin. She clutched the sheet with those claws and pulled it up under her chin. Her eyes were astonishingly bright. She looked at Stu and informed him for the third time that morning that her letters were all out.

Nancy, the young woman from hospice, had tried to explain. Stu could not expect sense from his mother now that she was moving into, what Nancy called, "this new stage of her life." The dying are already someplace else, she said, and really, that was okay. She had put a hand on Stu's arm and looked into his eyes. It was, she said, perfectly normal.

He didn't see why Nancy was trying to comfort him. He wasn't the one dying. She kept touching him and saying gentle, reassuring things. He didn't want any of that. What he wanted was his life back. His wife and daughter had moved out of the trailer a week ago to make room for Nancy, and Stu resented it. He wanted his family. He wanted his mother. But instead, everything was Nancy. Sometimes he wanted to grit his teeth and ask her who the hell she thought she was.

He bent down and kissed his mother's sunken cheek.

She looked up at him, and her forehead wrinkled. "My window . . ." But like so much she had tried to say in the last week, the sentence had no ending.

Stu felt a hand on his back. He closed his eyes and turned from the bed to kiss his wife. She avoided his lips, though, and pulled him into a hug. When she loosened her grip, Stu leaned back expecting deep, dark eyes. But it was Nancy in his arms—her eyes cool and blue, like something you might skate on.

"Thanks," he heard himself say. "Thank you."

*   *   *

In the shed behind the house, Stu put on his oilcloths and then made his way down to the dock. The tide was high, and the air was salty. He could not see Pressy's old crabbing boat through the fog, but he could smell it. No amount of washing or painting could ever rid old 247 of the reek of fish. How his wife hated that smell, and yet everything Stu did brought it home—the crabs, the pots, the bait, the boat, his clothes, his hands. JoAnna said it was a poor smell and she wanted more out of her life than that. Stu had loved that about JoAnna at first. She was better than he had ever expected he'd be able to do, and it had given him hope that if he worked hard he might make more of himself than he was.

The hull took shape as he got closer—battered, white, thirty feet long, and somewhat darker than the fog. Stu stepped aboard and started the diesel. He pumped the bilge, and then loaded a bushel of bait fish into the box. In ten minutes, he was headed down the creek toward the bay.

By the time the fog had lifted, he was far enough out that there was only a thin line of land between the sky and the water. At the crabbing grounds, Stu throttled down and steered for his line of floats. They were reassuring, those buoys. Wind and current might do as they liked, but still, his floats held their places and marked his traps. He snatched the first one, laid its line over the pulley, and wound it onto the spool. The winch growled, and the boat leaned. When the pot broke free of the mud and began to come up, the winch sang a happier song. Stu watched the line slip from its own reflection in the water. Then the wire-mesh of the crab trap broke the murk into small squares. And below, barely showing at first in the brown water, were the blue tips of carapace and claw. When the trap rose out of the water, crabs scuttled into the corners, claws upraised against whatever had brought them so rudely into the light. Stu hauled the trap into the boat, opened the lid. and shook crabs into the sorting bin. He re-baited and tossed the trap back. The line ran out after it. Then it was on to the next float and through the same routine one hundred and four more times that morning.

Always, the traps came up with angry crabs shimmering through the murk. And always, it amazed Stu that they could be so stupid, that they would continue to crawl into something they could not get out of. Why hadn't word spread through crab society—stay away from the wire mesh things? But it was greed. They came for the richest food on the bottom. They wanted the best and did not realize that the best always came at a high price.

Stu pointed the boat toward home and locked the wheel. He sorted through the crabs, separating the ones from the twos. Crabs tried to pinch him, but all he felt through his thick gloves was pressure, like a ring that was too tight. By the time he got to the dock, he had two dozen full baskets. Through the slats, he could see the white froth building as the crabs blew bubbles to protect their gills.

His daughter, Gloria, thought that crabs were having fun when they did that. But after Stu's mother came to die, Gloria changed. She asked where the man took the baskets full of crabs that Stu stacked in the shade of the shed. One day, she pulled the lids off a half dozen baskets and tried to get the crabs back into the water. Stu heard her scream, and by the time he got to her, crabs had clamped onto both of her hands and other crabs clamped onto those so that she trailed streamers of crabs from both arms and could not get them off. JoAnna cleaned the scratches and kissed the pinched places, but Gloria was inconsolable. She was going to die. No, JoAnna said. Yes, Gloria wailed. Daddy says. Everybody does. Grandpa, Grandma, him, you. And nobody will take care of me.

JoAnna had given Stu a look.

At the dock, he unloaded the baskets. He hosed the boat, washing bunker scales and stray claws into the bottom. Then he pumped the bilge and scooped out whatever pieces of crab he could find. Still many more, he knew, lodged under the floorboards where they would perpetuate the poor, dead smell that trailed behind Stu like a cloud.

He hung his oilcloths in the shed and headed for the house. Every morning after checking the crab pots, Stu stopped at the house just to see how things were. JoAnna would be at work, and Gloria at school. Then three days a week, he'd get in the truck and head up the creek to run Pressy's dredge. After that, it was back to the house for lunch. In the afternoon, he'd be on call at the salvage yard.

"Hellooo!" he called.

Just a few weeks earlier, his mother would have said, "Stu?" as if there was much of a chance that it would be somebody else. But today, the water was running, so his mother was in the shower. No. His mother was in the bed in the living room. It was Nancy in the shower. Stu stood there watching his mother sleep. Her forehead wrinkled, and her body stiffened with each inhalation. Life, she had always said, is what you put up with so you can get on to more important things. But when the cancer came upon her, she resisted, not so much to live but to keep from being killed. Thank God she had stopped asking Stu to heal her. Even if he'd had the power, he wouldn't have known whether healing for her lay in living or dying.

It was a relief to get into the truck. In fifteen minutes he was out of the willows and sycamores and up into the oaks and pines, up where there was no tide, no seagulls, and no smell of salt or dead fish. He turned onto a sandy road that wound back toward the creek. Here there was only the smell of pine needles and old oak leaves. The road ended in a clearing. Stu pulled the gangplank from the bed of the truck and dragged it to the riverside where the dredge was tied. The tall spuds and upraised cutter head made the machine look like some sort of insect.

The gangplank bounced as he walked across it. He started the little diesel and winched the dredge into the middle of the current. He dropped both spuds and felt them settle into the river bottom. The dredge was planted firm as a heron. It was good to feel grounded even with the current swirling all around, but here above the tide line, where the water flowed the same way, hour after day after for- ever, Stu felt a kind of draining away, an emptying. And he could never quite convince himself that there was enough rain and snow in the world to keep the rivers and creeks flowing.

He swept the cutter head across the bottom and sucked sand from the river for half an hour to replenish the pile from which Pressy supplied local contractors. Then he winched the dredge back to the shore, dropped both spuds, raised the head, and shut the diesel down.

On his way to the truck, he stopped at the separator to check the screens. In the summers, Gloria used to come with him. She liked to see what the dredge had brought up with the sand. Mostly it was driftwood and rocks. Sometimes bottles and cans, and every now and then bones. Once, a silver dollar. They made a game out of the driftwood, finding pieces that looked like things. But the last time Gloria came. everything looked dead to her—dead fish, dead bird, dead cloud.

It was hard on a ten-year-old. But what was Stu supposed to do? His mother was terrified of nursing homes, which they couldn't afford anyway. She wanted to stay with them, and how could you deny someone you loved something they wanted, especially when you wouldn't get many more chances to give them anything at all?

"She has to die to get to heaven," his wife told Gloria. "Sometimes things get bad so they can get better later on." JoAnna had looked at Stu, and he felt that he could see farther into the darkness of her eyes than usual. With his mother out of the way, life would be easier for JoAnna. There would be no one to judge her. "You're rich in the spirit," his mother used to tell him, "but your wife can't see it and doesn't care a thing about it." JoAnna knew that the old woman thought she was money-hungry and selfish, and JoAnna was determined to prove her wrong. So she lived in the trailer, breathing the poor smells she hated, and did not complain to anyone but Stu.

When his mother took to her bed permanently and began to lose touch with the world around, JoAnna said it was time for professional help. JoAnna could go back to her job, and they would find somebody to help them all. They interviewed four people hospice recommended, and JoAnna picked the young, married woman who lived just two miles down the road. When the woman asked what kind of accommodations they offered, JoAnna didn't miss a beat. "You can have our daughter's room," she said. "Gloria and I will be staying at my aunt's." Stu hadn't even thought about that, about where the woman would sleep, about how they would fit another person into the trailer. When JoAnna said she would be leaving, Stu didn't move or speak. He stared at her, unblinking, and he remembered thinking that if he didn't respond to what she had said, it might never sink in and things would go on as they always had. JoAnna returned his stare. The silence stretched out between them, and the news began to fade. It might have disappeared altogether if JoAnna hadn't wavered, if a moment of regret or guilt hadn't flitted across her face. She shifted her weight and looked away from him, and when she looked back again, he could see—she was gone.

From the separator, Stu picked a piece of driftwood that looked like a horn of plenty. Instead of fruit spilling out, though, it had all sorts of animals—deer, bird, groundhog, turtle, snake. It had nothing to do with death. Gloria would see. He put it on the dashboard of the truck and headed up the sandy road toward the blacktop, and then back toward the trailer for lunch.

His mother was asleep. Or at least she was not awake. Morphine had wrapped its blanket around her. Under it, she seemed unperturbed, warm. Stu thought he would probably like morphine. He ate a sandwich but did not want any soup. Nancy sat on the couch with the television turned down low and a magazine opened on her lap.

"What does he think about you staying here?" Stu said. They had talked about Nancy's husband before. Stu could not understand what sort of marriage they must have when she spent days and weeks living in other people's houses. It made Stu feel better, though, knowing that he was not the only one who had been left alone.

"Who can tell?" said Nancy. "He hasn't given me that lesson yet."

Her husband was a teacher, and to hear her tell it, life with him was all correction and instruction and never being quite good enough.

"I like working," she said. "He can't criticize if he doesn't see what I'm doing. Plus, I meet people."

"So you just stay gone?"

"I work here or somewhere. It'll all smooth out. I don't give up on us, but I don't force it, either."

Wasn't it her job to help people give up, to make empty arms easier, to somehow endure?

Stu sat on the other end of the couch waiting for the call to work. A lot of junkyard work was waiting. Days would go by with Pressy sitting in the office, his greasy boots propped up on his greasy desk listening to the plaintive calls of the parts service radio.

Stu had taken the job determined to work and save his way out. That was when he and JoAnna were still on track—still headed toward the same place. But the longer he stayed at the yard, the more he knew he liked it.

It was the stillness. All those cars, all that movement brought to a stop. But not dead, not useless. You pulled necessary things from them.

"My letters . . ." his mother said.

Stu got up off the couch and stood over her. She was looking at the ceiling and gripping the sheet. She pulled it toward her chin with all her depleted might.

Nancy bathed his mother's face with a damp washcloth. Stu caught his mother's eye, but she looked at him from a great distance.

They cut themselves off, Nancy had said. Little by little, they give up friends, family, food. They have to, she said. And it was okay.

The phone rang, and Pressy's gravelly voice said, simply, "Parts."

Stu kissed his mother on the forehead and left the trailer. He got into the pickup, where the horn of plenty was drying nicely on the dash, and he headed out the drive and across the creek toward the yard. It was a three minute drive, but if he had been able to walk on water he could have been there in half that. He parked inside the gate and walked to the office. Pressy grinned. "Fresh meat," he said.

It was what Stu liked least about the job—a new wreck. Pressy had inventoried what was good on it, and now Stu had to hitch it up behind the tractor and drag it into the yard and find a place for it. He frowned.

Pressy raised his eyebrows. His nostrils flared. "Trouble?"

"No," Stu said.

Pressy knew Stu's mother was dying; he knew that JoAnna and Gloria were staying in town, too. Probably, he thought he knew more than that.

"We're in the right business," Pressy said. "Every single thing in this life breaks down, wears out, or winds up wrecked. We'll always have work, huh?"

Stu grunted and went outside to get the tractor. He backed it up in front of the wreck, which, as near as he could tell, had once been a Firebird. The crash had pushed the dashboard back into the front seats, but amazingly, the radio was still playing. Stu hooked a chain to the mangled front end and set off dragging the carcass up the hill. He found a space for it near the other Pontiacs and unhooked the chain. That radio bothered him. He forced the door open far enough to reach inside. Part of a fast food hamburger lay near its wrapper on the floor. If he looked closer he knew he might find other things too—fingers or feet, perhaps. The off button on the radio did not work, so Stu rode away on the tractor, leaving the Firebird to sing itself to sleep. The battery would die in a while. Mice would find the food and whatever else needed to be gotten rid of. Lizards would move in, and wasps would build nests. Dust would settle like a shroud, and then the Firebird would belong. It would stay there for years, giving up a part every so often.

Stu parked the tractor in the shed behind the office and walked down the hill toward the river. He breathed the pungent smells of the yard—the weeds, the old motor oil, the rotting upholstery. Cicadas buzzed. It was good to be alive, to breathe the air and hear the sounds.

His mother was in pain, but she clung to life. Stu didn't blame her. She had lost so much by dwelling on rumors about the next world. Stu would not make that mistake. Stu would cling to certainties.

Near the river, the air was cooler, and here, where the tide came and went, the dead fish and mud smells filled him with hope. His stomach grumbled. He drew a deep breath. How many times a day did he breathe, and how many breaths in a lifetime? Still, when you took the time to notice, each one was wonderful. Stu found his fishing pole beneath the willow tree, and he took a seat in the old kitchen chair. He dug around in the bait can that had been there more than a week. There were still plenty of worms. The one he chose writhed on the hook. Stu wiped his fingers on his pants and swung the line over the water and in. He hoped he would get no bites, though. All he wanted was to watch the river flow until the tide was out. He wanted each minute to go by identically to the previous ones until the tide changed and the water moved the other way and it was quitting time, when he could drive home to his trailer, the roof of which he could see from where he sat.

There was no more work that day, and at five, Stu stood up and drew his bare hook from the water. He leaned the pole against the willow and walked back up the hill. The chain on the dog pen clattered, and Death and Plunder howled out into the yard like hounds on a trail. At any minute, he could step from behind a wreck and face them. There would be a tense testing of wills. No matter how many times Stu had backed them down, they had never warmed to him, had never learned to leave him alone. But the dogs must have gone to some other corner of the yard, for Stu did not see them. He got into his truck and headed home.

The Buick was there, parked next to Nancy's Escort, so Stu pulled onto the sparse grass he had coaxed from the sandy soil. He switched off the key and took the horn of plenty from the dash.

Nancy was bent over his mother's bed trying to get her to eat something. JoAnna was on the couch, her hands in her lap like someone in a waiting room. She stood when Stu walked in and held both hands out to him. He could only take one, though, because the horn of plenty was in the other. She leaned forward and kissed him not quite on the lips.

Gloria came from her room. "She moved my animals," the girl said. "I want to take them home."

"Hey, honey," Stu said. He hugged his daughter, pulling her against his hip. "This *is* home," he said. "And as soon as . . ." But he stopped because he couldn't find anything in what there was to say that should be said. He bent down and held out the horn of plenty. "Look what I dredged up for us today."

Gloria took it from him. Her eyes got that empty look she sometimes had, and her mouth hung open.

"Shut that mouth," her mother said.

Gloria had heard it a million times—a slack mouth makes a child look dumb. JoAnna was afraid that Gloria was not quite right. Stu said they should relax and just take the child like she was, but JoAnna would not settle for that. Something drove her. Something about hope. His mother had lived for it, too, carrying her soul like a fetus, always expecting the body to crack open and the spirit to fly. But hope hurt, Stu knew. It was better not to have than to lose.

"Well," Stu said to Gloria, "what is it?"

"Wood," the girl said. "Smells."

Stu straightened up. Could she have forgotten their game already? Or was it just that they were not at the river, not standing in sand and smelling the smells that went with the game?

Nancy finished with his mother, who had eaten nothing. "Ready for dinner?" she asked them.

Gloria nodded and gave the horn of plenty back to Stu.

They sat at the kitchen table. Nancy took a tuna casserole from the oven and peas and potatoes from the stove. It felt like they were in somebody else's house, or at a restaurant. Nancy made herself a tray and carried it to her room so the family could have some time alone. Still, it was not comfortable. Stu's mother might be able to hear and understand everything, and so they could not talk about her, about the one subject that eclipsed every other.

Gloria finished first and asked if she could go get some of her stuffed animals. JoAnna nodded. Then they could hear Nancy talking to the girl. "Sure," she said, "they're yours, honey, and this is still your room. I'm just staying here for a while, you know? I'm taking good care of them, but I had to take them off the bed because I'm bigger than you are."

Normally, Stu would not have asked. Normally, he would have acted like he always did and would have hoped that the rest of the world would do the same. But he couldn't help himself. "Why was she doing that?"

"What?" JoAnna said.

"Taking her animals."

JoAnna put down her fork and swallowed. "She wants her things."

"Can't you tell her?" Stu glanced over his shoulder toward the living room. "Can't you tell her that she'll be back, that it won't be long?"

JoAnna leaned on her elbows and lowered her voice. "You know what I see when I look at that girl, Stu? I see me, but it's like I've caught something that makes me slow and lazy."

"You can't tell her?"

"Staying at Jane's, now, it's funny. I don't feel that way so much. And Gloria seems to be coming out of herself. You can't see it because she gets weird when she's back here, but I see it."

JoAnna got up and cleared the table. She washed the dishes, and Stu dried. He always dried and put away. It was a good feeling to neaten up after a meal, but it was different now. Even after he had wiped off the table and hung up the dishtowel, the trailer felt cluttered and full of unfinished business.

His mother groaned, and JoAnna went to her bedside. "It's okay, Mom. We'll be back. Maybe you'll be better tomorrow."

"Tomorrow."

"Yes," JoAnna said, and she bent over and kissed Stu's mother on the forehead. Gloria touched her lips to the dying woman's cheek and then turned away and buried her face in her stuffed animal, in the softness of things that would not die.

"Say goodbye to Daddy."

Gloria reached out an arm and hugged Stu. "Bye, Daddy."

Stu found that he could not say, "Goodbye, honey."

JoAnna and Gloria piled into the Buick, and the taillights disappeared up the road.

His mother groaned. She opened her eyes and searched the ceiling. "What do they want?" she said.

Nancy came out of her room. She had on her house-coat. "What?"

His mother groaned again. The sound came from deep in her throat.

"Morphine?" Nancy said.

"Tomorrow," his mother said.

"What about it, Mom?"

His mother's eyes seemed to take in the room, Stu, Nancy. She seemed to pull light into herself and to shine with it.

Stu wanted to ask his mother what she thought he ought to do. But his eyes were hot, and his lips could not make words.

Nancy took his hand and led him into the kitchen. She backed him around the corner so they were out of sight of his mother. Her arms went around him.

Stu wished he had arms enough to hold everything—his wife, his daughter, his mother.

"What am I supposed to do?" he said.

Nancy looked at him. The cool blue of her eyes made him feel exposed, as if he was out on the ice somewhere. Her face tilted upward, and she smiled a sad smile.

She was so different. She was a force grinding away at what he knew. But what confused him was that he wanted, more than anything right then, to kiss her.

The Mercy of the World

Out through the windshield, from the direction that should have been down, a scattering of stars shined up at Stu, as if space was a bottomless pit. It made him woozy. Hanging in his seatbelt with his foot pressing desperately on the brake, it still felt like the car was tumbling. Stu squeezed the wheel and managed to find himself in the rearview mirror. It steadied him, somehow, this vision of his head haloed by the red glow of brake lights.

His friend, Brody, lay on the car's ceiling, and his voice came to Stu as if from on high. "Satisfied?" it said.

Stu had been driving far too fast. Even in the curves, he had kept his foot on the gas so that the Civic slid sideways on the dirt road and its tires spun stones into the dark woods. He was drunk on Nancy. Six months since they had started whatever it was they had going, he was still full-to-bursting with her.

She had invited them for dinner as thanks for their help earlier that day when they had all picked her vegetables until there were no more boxes or bags left to put them in. Stu and Brody had finally sat in the shade and watched Nancy continue to work, filling a laundry basket with tomatoes for Stu to take home. She wore shorts and a cut-off tee shirt that showed her flat stomach, shiny with sweat. When Stu told her not to give him more than she could spare, she stood and shrugged. Her hands seemed almost to cup her breasts. "I've got plenty," she had said.

Brody shook his head. "Mmph," was all he had managed to say. For him, Nancy was a spectator sport.

Once the basket was full, Stu and Brody loaded it into the Civic and drove back to Stu's place. They set the basket in the shed, and Stu carried a few tomatoes into the trailer. Most would go to waste. He would throw them on the compost heap, where even then, they'd be a waste because Nancy had so much to spare that Stu had not even bothered to plant a garden of his own this year.

Brody sat at the kitchen table and ignored the beer Stu put before him. He had a tomato in each hand, and he could hardly contain himself. Red and yellow peeked from between his fingers. "Sweetest things under that little shirt of hers," he said. "I wanted to go down on my knees. Wanted to say, 'Thank you, Lordy, for the fruits of this earth.'"

Stu smiled. He was blessed. He downed a beer and opened another. It would be sweet to tell the world, but Nancy was a secret. She would never leave her husband. She had made that very clear. And that was good, she had said, because if Stu never really had her, why then he would never really be able to lose her, either. In that respect, she said, she would be better than a wife. They had both smiled. JoAnna had left Stu almost a year ago, and so, yes, Nancy was far better than that.

"All I saw you do," Stu said to Brody, "was sit in the dirt of that garden and eat onions right out of the ground."

"It was all I could do," Brody said, "to keep my soul from flying right out of my body."

Stu shook his head. "When it comes to Nancy, a man," he said, "needs to be able to get to his body good and quick."

"Humph," said Brody. "What man would that be?"

Stu's smile had a life of its own. How could you keep a secret that felt like good news?

Brody winced and set his tomato breasts aside. He leaned forward and frowned. A question, *the* question, was forming itself in those eyes.

It felt to Stu like the first time you see a photo of yourself with a new girlfriend. The showing made it real. But this girl was not his, and so Stu grabbed another beer and carried it with him to the bathroom. He drank it down and got in the shower where he tried to push away the guilt. When he emerged from the bathroom, Brody was brooding at the table, his fingers linked around his beer, as if in prayer.

Stu opened another can and downed it. Then he roused Brody, and they went out to the Civic. Brody folded his long legs into the little car, and sat there, that frown still on his face and his whole body hunched like a question mark.

Stu drove like a crazy man, a half-wild secret whipping him on. When they seemed close to tumbling out of control, Brody twisted in his seat as if body English could help. "Hup, ho!" he said. But Stu was too drunk, too happy about the thought of Nancy to slow down. And so, when the front wheels hit whatever it was in the road, the Civic rose into the air and turned end over end, lightly and silently, like an acrobat. Brody managed only a single "God!" before the car came down on its roof and slid to a stop in the ditch, and everything was quiet except for Brody, who wanted to know if Stu was satisfied. "Because if you're not," he said, "maybe we can go on up the road and see if we can wreck a house too."

"Not wrecked," Stu said, dangling in his seat. "Just upside-down, is all."

"Pfft," Brody said. He crawled out the passenger side window and stood with his head hanging toward the stars. "You ought not go to this dinner," he said, "because, if you ask me, somebody is trying to tell you something."

Stu hung there, hands on the wheel, foot on the bake. "Which somebody?" he said.

"Come on," said Brody, "before the blood goes to your head and you start to get ideas."

Stu pressed the button on the seatbelt and let himself down to the ceiling. He knew what he needed. He needed Nancy—the one person in the world who knew who he really was. He crawled out the window and stood. Everything was right-side-up again, but still Stu felt dizzy, somehow, and turned around.

*   *   *

Jason's hounds started to bay as soon as they heard Stu and Brody coming up the driveway. The sound was sweet to Stu's ears, and he made Brody stop and listen to the howls echo through the woods. It reminded Stu of the dogs his father used to keep, and he had that feeling again of expectation—of some wild thing they would bring from the darkness.

"Gives me the creeps," Brody said.

"Yeah," said Stu. "Beautiful."

Nancy was at the back door when the two came onto the porch. Stu stepped into the light first, and Nancy smiled as if she wasn't surprised one bit, as if she had known all along what the hounds were sounding about. Her smile was a complicated thing. The lips turned down at the corners even when she was happiest.

Brody pulled open the screen door and let Stu go in. The kitchen was warm and full of the smells of dinner. Green beans and carrots were steaming, chicken was frying, and a blackberry pie cooled on the counter.

"Didn't hear you drive up," Nancy said.

Brody came in and let the door shut behind him. "That's because we flew part of the way," he said.

"Where's your car?"

"Dead in the ditch," Brody said. "Laying on its back with its feet in the air."

The smile left Nancy's face. "Accident?" she said.

"No," Brody said. "I think somebody's trying to tell the man something, myself." He looked at Stu and winked.

"Brody," Stu said. "Shut up."

Jason was sitting at the little table against the far wall in the dining room, cutting letters into a sign with a wood-burning tool. He was tall and prematurely gray at the temples. He had big, deep-set eyes that he rarely leveled at anyone. Stu thought it was the same kind of caution a good hunter uses when he avoids carelessly pointing a gun.

Jason turned in his chair. "Come on," he said, "let's hear it."

"Yeah," said Brody. "Let's hear the story."

Stu was not sure what to say. He would have liked to fall into Nancy's arms and be soothed and told that he was not a bad thing, not a homewrecker. But Nancy's back was to him. She was turning the chicken, and Stu suffered a moment of panic as he wondered who she was.

"I'm not too sure where it starts," he said.

"Well . . ." Brody sniffed the pie. "You can just skip over all that stuff about the night when you were made and about how much your momma wished she'd had a headache."

Jason turned back to his sign. It read, "Jason and Nancy Jackson." The "Jason an" was already burned into the wood, but the rest was just outlined in pencil, neat and sharp. "How drunk *are* you?" he said.

"Mmm-hmm," said Brody. "Now we're getting closer to the start of the story."

"I'm a little bit drunk," Stu said.

"That's right," said Brody. He leaned over Jason's shoulder and watched him work. "And you better watch out too, because some day he might come flying down your road and flip his car right on top of your mailbox. Probably wipe this pretty little sign right out!"

Jason frowned at his work. A little curl of smoke rose off the "d" at the end of "and."

*   *   *

Nancy started the chicken around the table for the second time even though the beans hadn't been around once yet. "Can't you pull it out with the tractor?" she said.

"Pass the beans, will you?" Jason said. "I already got chicken. Everybody got chicken."

Nancy lifted the bread and sent it around. "Tractor'd do, wouldn't it?"

"Tractor isn't running," Jason said. "Transmission case is cracked. Pass the beans."

"Is that bad?" Nancy said.

"Pass the beans."

"Is that, like, a disease—transmission case?"

Jason stretched across the table and picked up the bowl of beans. "The tractor is not running," he said.

The beans went around the table, but when they came back to Nancy, she passed them on to Jason again. "How about the truck?"

Jason set the beans down. "Truck won't pull it out," he said. "Not upside down and in a ditch."

"How do you know," Nancy said, "unless you try? Pass the beans, please."

Jason stared at her. Most people thought he was a good husband. Came right home after work. Did little projects around the house. Didn't drink. Didn't throw his money around, and didn't throw himself around either. He was just loyal and true. Not that he had to be. Stu knew for a fact that a number of women were interested in him. But it was as if Jason had looked at the angles and had seen that being true was the best shot, and so he made up his mind that true was the way it was going to be, and there he was. The man's mind, Stu knew, was a hundred times stronger than his body.

And that was part of the problem, because Nancy was made the other way around. She didn't care much about how things were supposed to be, she just was, and that was as right as it got for her. Maybe it was a little tangled, like vines in the woods, but you couldn't say the woods were wrong just because they weren't laid out like lawns. You could see the tangle in the way she cooked. Seemed like she wandered on to the next step before the first one was done. But the food was always fine, and everything was hot. And good. Stu took chicken to his mouth—a man hadn't eaten until he sat at Nancy's table.

Of course, if that had been the only thing wrong between Nancy and Jason, they would have been able to work it out themselves. Each of them would have found a way to fill in the other's missing parts. But it was worse than that, because there was something in Nancy that thought Jason was right about her. It was the part of her that thought she didn't have a good mind, the part that thought she ought to be somebody different from who she was.

Women were like that sometimes, Stu thought, like they aren't sure where they stop and other people start. Stu knew Nancy felt ashamed of herself and that sometimes she would not have minded just disappearing. Probably, she had no idea why she was having an affair with Stu. She just felt like something was wrong, and she was glad for somebody to take her the way she was. Thinking with her heart, but you couldn't tell Stu that the woman wasn't smart.

"The beans?" Nancy repeated. Her hand was out, waiting for the bowl.

Jason handed it to her. "I know that the truck will not pull this man's car out of the ditch," he said, looking her straight in the eye, "because I am thinking. Because I am not just wandering around in my head like some dream."

Nancy took the bowl and bowed her head over it.

Stu watched her scoop food onto her plate, and his heart grew light. The alcohol seemed to warm him and buoy him up. If it weren't for Stu, Jason would have squeezed Nancy right out of existence. There'd be nothing left but a bad imitation of Jason. Maybe she was cheating, Stu thought, but, strange as it was to imagine, cheating was saving her marriage. It made Stu smile. He chewed food cooked by Jason's wife, and for the first time in almost a year, he didn't feel guilty. He was helping them. The food tasted better, and he swallowed easier. He belonged. They needed him. Stu smiled at the beans on his plate. He was not a bad thing. He was just doing what he could to help.

If there had been someone like him around when his own marriage was on the rocks, his wife might have stayed. He could have learned to accept her need for work and money; he could have adjusted to the men she befriended and to the power she loved. He could have done it all if she had just been happy enough to stay.

Nancy was staring at her plate, loading beans onto her fork and dumping them off again.

"What's the matter," Jason was saying, "no more ideas about how to get the car out of the ditch? Maybe we could all go down and pray it out. Or lay hands on it." He grinned. "You leave the thinking to me, okay? And I'll leave the dreaming to you."

Nancy said nothing.

"What you're going to need," Jason said to Stu, "is a tow truck."

"But that's so expensive," Nancy said. "I don't see how you know what he needs unless you've seen where his car is."

"He *told* me where it is."

The words were coming from Stu's lips before he even knew he was going to speak. "What would you two do," he heard himself say, "if I wasn't around to referee? Huh?" He looked at Jason. "Ever think about that?"

Jason sat back in his seat. His eyebrows plowed together, and he seemed unable to focus on the question.

Nancy looked down at her plate and fidgeted with the chicken.

Brody, who had been shoveling food into his mouth as if he was afraid someone was going to take his plate away before he was finished, stopped chewing. His empty fork was in midair. He lowered it, adjusting himself in his chair, selected chicken instead of beans and began to eat again, slowly, as if a quick move might tip the whole world.

"I mean . . ." Stu could not seem to find his place. "I mean, what if I didn't love both of you the best way I knew how?"

Jason shifted his perplexed look to Nancy, but she would not meet his eye. "The trouble with a tow truck," Jason said, his voice level, "is that the man's going to have to call the cops."

"Utt oh," said Brody.

"So?" said Nancy. "So what?"

"Relax. They'll just want to know what happened, is all." Jason aimed his eyes at Stu. "Might give our friend here a drunk test, too."

"Oh, that's okay," Brody said. "He'll pass that just fine. He's plenty drunk."

"Brody," Nancy said, "can't you shut up?"

"Might lose his license," Jason said. "Might not be able to come up and down this road for a while."

Nancy put her fork down. She smoothed the napkin in her lap and raised her eyes to meet Jason's.

"Don't get mad at me," he said. "It's not my fault." He smiled and the look on his face reminded Stu of a man hefting a new weapon. "Why don't you serve dessert, honey? Brody hasn't had a bite in a minute now, and he might die of hunger." Jason turned to Stu. "And looks like you maybe want something sweeter."

Stu shrugged.

"You know," Jason said, "I don't really like blackberry pie. No matter how much sugar you put in, those blackberries are still bitter."

*   *   *

Stu and Brody stood by the dog pen waiting for Jason. He was still in the kitchen, standing behind Nancy, talking while she did the dishes. Stu caught the tones of the conversation that came through the open window. Jason was angry and earnest. Nancy was flustered and defensive.

The dogs were beside themselves. Five of them shared the pen, and they crowded the fence where Stu and Brody stood. Their tails wagged, and their bodies wiggled. They reminded Stu of sperm.

For all their eagerness, though, Jason's dogs were the laughing stock of the county. Stu would have liked to drag out some of the stories about them tracking for hours and then "barking treed" around a garbage can, but he couldn't get his mind off what was going on in the house.

Finally, Jason let the screen door slam behind him and strode across the yard. His eyes seemed to cut right through the darkness.

"We were just admiring these fine dogs you got here," Brody said.

Jason was not amused. "Well, I've got a feeling that tonight they'll find something worth finding." He opened the gate, and the dogs bounded out of the pen and scattered into the dark woods, barking and howling.

Jason got into his car, and Stu and Brody piled in after him. A mile down the road they rounded a curve, and the night was suddenly alive with lights. The tow truck's spinning yellows turned the woods an eerie green. Beyond were the swirling blues of a state cop. The tow truck shone its work light, revealing the underside of Stu's car all greasy and tubey, like the guts of some animal, just the way Brody had said, dead in the ditch.

"Mmph!" Brody said. "Looks like Judgment Day."

"Shut up, Brody," Stu said.

"All right," Brody said, and he got out of the car. "I'm going to go help the man put things right."

Stu's heart beat in his throat. His mouth was dry. He felt suddenly drunker than ever as he sat there silently with Jason and watched Brody talk to the cop. He didn't want to talk to the man himself, not until he sobered up, not until the world stopped spinning.

The cop poked around in the weeds by Stu's car. He picked up an empty beer can and showed it to Brody. Brody shook his head. The cop said something. Brody shook his head again and pointed toward Jason's car.

"Oh man," Stu said.

Jason turned to him. "What're you going to tell him?"

"Don't know."

"Know what I'd do if I was you?" Jason said.

"What's that?"

"If I was you . . ." Jason narrowed his eyes. His face was sometimes blue, sometimes yellow, sometimes green in the chaotic lights. "If I was you, I'd lie."

Jason's dogs were not far off, howling as if they had struck trail. It was an urgent, joyful sort of sadness. And that music would get sadder and sadder the closer they got to what they were after until they would stand under a tree somewhere and cry so hard that it seemed whatever they had found would break their hearts if they ever managed to catch it.

"Think what you want," Stu said, "but I'm no liar."

Jason shook his head. "Lying's not the problem," he said. "Unless you can lie, you're just at the mercy of the world. Tell him a coon dog ran out in front of you and you swerved to miss it. No reckless driving, no drunk test, no ticket." Jason turned away and looked out the windshield at the flashing night.

"I'm not out to hurt anybody," Stu said. "I'm trying to help."

"See there?" Jason said. "Now, there's a lie. But it's a good one. You ought to try living up to that."

Brody left the cop and crossed the road to Jason's car. His hand shaded his eyes and he squinted down looking for his footing. "Man wants to talk to you, Stu."

"All right," Stu said. He stepped out of the car and walked toward the cruiser. The lights swirled around him, making it seem, sometimes, as if there was nothing beneath him at all. In the woods nearby, Jason's dogs howled.

The cop pointed to the passenger door, and Stu got in. The interior light was on and the clipboard in the man's lap held a form. Some machine on the dash flashed a number, and the radio crackled with static. The cop reached out and turned it down.

"What happened here?" he said.

Stu tried to remember what it had been like flying through the air and landing in the ditch. He opened his mouth to speak, but nothing was there. He could find only broken bits of memory.

Truth was, he had been too drunk to be driving.

The dogs howled in the darkness.

Truth was, knowing Nancy was a cheater had made it easier for Stu to deal with losing JoAnna. It had made him feel that no woman was worth having, that family was just an illusion.

"Sir?" said the cop. "Are you all right?"

"Yes," Stu said, but he did not know what to tell the man.

The cop's radio stuttered some message Stu could not make out. The man reached forward and turned it down again. He looked at Stu. His face was sharp and suspicious.

"It was a dog," Stu said. "A coon dog ran in front of me, and I swerved."

The cop turned away. He stared into the night with the empty look of someone who was listening. The dark was alive with the music of the dogs. He listened for a while. Then he nodded over his clipboard and filled out the form. When it was finished, he handed it to Stu for his signature.

It was only a warning. Where it said, "I certify that these statements are true," Stu wrote his name. Then he stepped from the cruiser clutching his copy. Jason came to stand with him, and they watched the tow truck pull his car from the ditch and set it on its wheels again. The windshield was webbed with cracks, and the roof was dented, but Stu would be able to get it on the road again.

"What'd you tell him?" Jason asked.

"A lie," Stu said. He supposed they were all lying up worlds for themselves.

Jason's face was yellow, then blue, then green in the lights. The muscles in his jaw worked for a moment before he nodded.

The Visitation

S tu had tried to convince himself that he could still be who he once had been, but as he stood in the trees behind a little beach on the Green River and watched his daughter step into the water, he saw, finally, that the girl had grown beyond him. She wore a long, white dress that ballooned out around her legs as she waded deeper into the river, and the man she was headed toward wore a coat and tie even though he was standing thigh-deep in the current. No, too many things had gone on in this child's world, things Stu did not understand.

A few weeks after JoAnna left him for another man and moved across the state, the paperwork arrived from her lawyer claiming that Stu was not Gloria's father. It was a lie. But the very fact that JoAnna had told it somehow set Stu adrift. He would much rather have paid child support than be cut off like that. Almost a year passed before he collected his wits enough to hire a lawyer and try to fight. It was a mere divorce, the lawyer reassured him. It was not a murder; it was not a gene transplant. It took another two years, but the guy proved Stu's paternity and won him visitation rights. But still, Stu felt like a ghost standing there in the trees, watching a girl he no longer knew. The divorce had not been a "mere" anything. What it had been, he thought, was an unmaking.

When Gloria reached the man, she took his hand and turned to face the shore. Her dress was soaked now, and it hung heavily from her shoulders. The man said a prayer to God the Forgiver, the Purifier, the Maker of New Beginnings. Then he wrapped Gloria in his arms and leaned her backwards, as if for a kiss. Her long, dark hair floated on the water for a moment before the man lowered her and the river closed over her face. Stu watched her disappear. He felt himself leaning forward. There was a catch in his throat, but he was not at all surprised to find that he had no idea what to do or even how to feel.

After a moment, the man lifted Gloria and helped her stand. Her dress stuck to her body like a second skin. Stu could see that her breasts were taut from the cold. The teenage boys at the back of the little group there on the beach must have seen it too because they craned their necks, and Stu heard one of them whisper, "Ho baby!"

The preacher helped her to shore, and she stood there, tall and shapely. She picked at her dress, pulling the cloth away from her body, but as soon as she let go, it clung again. She folded her arms across her chest and frowned. Her eyes, which used to hide beneath half closed lids that sometimes made her seem dim, were dark and mysterious now.

"Praise God," the man said. He swept the air with his hand. "Purified."

"A-*men!*" said that boy in the back of the group.

JoAnna stepped forward and draped a towel over Gloria's shoulders. The girl held it closed in front like a shawl, and people started to gather around. Men stepped up to shake Gloria's hand, and women hugged her, leaning out to keep from getting themselves wet. Only the boys hung back, unable, it seemed, to trust themselves. And Stu stayed back, too.

He had wanted to get there earlier in the day so he could talk to Gloria before the people came, but that hadn't worked out. He had fussed and worried. First, it was his clothes. It was just like him to spend over a year working toward this visit, but then not to consider what he'd wear until the day was on him. JoAnna said the ceremony would be outside, and so he should wear casual clothes, but he didn't trust her. He put on his best pants. His best shirt was missing a button, but he covered that up with a tie. His old sport jacket needed pressing, but the biggest problem was his shoes. All he had were boots and tennis shoes. He tried them all, standing on a chair each time so he could see what they looked like in the mirror. Finally, he settled on a pair of black boots that were relatively clean because they were too small and he had not worn them much.

Then, at the end of his four-hour drive, he had gotten lost, or at least he thought he was lost. The fence that bordered JoAnna's property stretched for half a mile and the fancy gate seemed to say that his battered old truck did not belong there.

He had gone wrong, so he turned around and retraced his path to a landmark he was sure of. Then he followed the directions again, but they brought him back to the same place. The gate was open, and Stu drove in, not stopping to think because he knew that if he stopped he might not go through with it.

The driveway rose through a grove of trees and then leveled off. Large pasture fields opened on either side, and to the west, Stu saw the mountains, a hazy dark blue against the sky. As he went higher, other mountains appeared behind the first. They reminded him of the bay in stormy weather—waves beyond waves. For a moment, the view made him forget himself. Then the driveway wound into another grove, and Stu saw the house.

He had been surprised when JoAnna said that the baptism would be outside at her place. It didn't seem like the woman he had known. But once he saw the house and the grounds, he realized that she was the same as she had ever been.

Stu pulled onto the grass of the pasture field where the other cars were parked, but he took a spot far from the rest. Even though he had blasted his truck with the pressure washer until the paint had started to peel, the bed still stank of dead fish. He shut off the engine, and when he got out of the truck, his feet sank into the rich grass.

The service had already started by the time he found the path and got to the beach. He walked quietly to the edge of the trees where he could look down at the little group and not be seen. The Green River curved beneath huge sycamores, whose branches met overhead like rafters. The sun had sunk below the hills, and twilight was already gathering under the trees.

Everyone was dressed casually. JoAnna had told him the truth about that, but it was expensive casual. Stu would have taken his tie off, but there was that missing button.

The preacher had one of those voices that could be in your ear without quite making it to your brain, so it took a moment for Stu to even realize that the guy was talking. He asked the congregation to sing "Shall We Gather at the River," and they did, reading the words from sheets of paper.

When the hymn was done, the preacher stepped into the water, wincing and struggling to keep his balance. He held his hand out for Gloria, and she stepped in after him and was baptized.

The preacher thanked God for the river and the day and for the rebirth of Gloria.

*   *   *

They sang "Amazing Grace," reading the words from the other side of the sheet. "Amen," the preacher said, finally, and then, with a kind of smirk, "let's eat."

Stu stood there among the trees watching people congratulate Gloria and then straggle away up the hill toward the house and food. Behind him, he could hear boys running in the darkening woods. He sensed they, too, were waiting for Gloria.

He could still leave. No one had even noticed he was there yet. In a way, Stu supposed, he wasn't there. But then JoAnna raised her head as if she had felt eyes upon her. She was still beautiful—dark-eyed and slender. Her yellow dress came to her knees, and she was barefoot in the sand. She fixed Stu in her gaze, but her eyes, in which he used to be able to lose himself, were flinty, now, and impenetrable.

"Hello, Stu," she said.

He stepped from the trees and made his way down.

"I was beginning to think you wouldn't make it." JoAnna looked him up and down, her eyes resting for a blink too long on his shoes. "You look the same as ever." She seemed satisfied with Stu, as if he were exactly what she wanted him to be. Same as ever. It was not a compliment, but Stu said thank you anyway.

"Say hello to your birth-dad, Gloria."

Gloria's forehead wrinkled, but she smiled. "Hey, b-dad. I've been reborn."

"Yes," Stu said. "I saw."

The three of them stood there in a triangle with nothing between them but the sound of cicadas. Finally, JoAnna suggested that Stu and Gloria walk to the house together. "Is that okay?" JoAnna said to Gloria. "Are you cold?"

Gloria was not cold. They would walk.

Stu watched JoAnna's car bounce away across the pas- ture field and up the hill. Then he turned toward Gloria. Willowy—that was the word for her.

Boys ran through the woods and hooted.

Gloria shook her head and rolled her eyes. "Not worth dirt," she said.

It was a relief to have a subject. "No?" Stu said.

"No."

He started them walking. "Must be some nice ones."

"Huh!" Gloria said. "Nice ones are the worst. Nice ones think they can get away with it."

"With?"

Gloria shrugged. "You know."

This was water much deeper than Stu had expected. "You're too young," he heard himself say. "Way too young to date."

"Well, they still come around," she said. "Dumb and dirty. And any-how, I'm not too young. I'm fourteen. It's just that I know better than Mom does who I ought to date."

"Right," Stu said. "After all, what does she know about this sort of stuff?"

"Really," Gloria said, and then she smiled.

She might have gotten his joke, even though it was not funny. How easy to make bad choices. How bad JoAnna's and his had been—foolish, shallow, hurtful—all because JoAnna thought he looked a certain way and that she might make something of him. And all because JoAnna came from a certain farming family that Stu thought would be an improvement over pulpwood and crabs. All because of a pregnancy. But there stood Gloria, slender and tall, soon to be a woman—the result of bad choices and misshaped dreams. He searched the girl's eyes, dark eyes that were his ex-wife's.

She turned her face toward the top of the hill. "Everything's got to be her way," Gloria said. "This guy wasn't even the preacher I wanted. And my girlfriends are too trashy to be invited."

They trudged onward, leaving the twilight of the river bottom and heading upward toward day. Stu noticed, with satisfaction, that they were in step.

"I wanted Mr. Jenkins, but Momma said that it was bad enough being baptized at my age, and worse that it had to be in a river, but she was absolutely not going to have a screamer there. That's what she calls him—a screamer. But he makes you feel it." Gloria's eyes narrowed to slits. "Like God's got you by the back of your neck," she said. "All power and glory. Gives you chills." She stopped walking and searched Stu's eyes, "You know?"

He knew. And it was better proof than blood tests that she was his.

When he was young, he too had a hold on God and could heal. It was an illusion, of course—just a childish hope that some powerful being somewhere cared, was looking out for him. As he grew up and things went wrong, the God feeling gradually disappeared. But he wanted to hug his daughter and tell her that he knew how she felt and that he hoped she could hold onto it.

"This guy today," Gloria said, "he was all yak yak, like God's just some idea he's got."

She was so grown up. Maybe she was too old to hug her father. Maybe she didn't even feel that he was her father.

"Well," Stu said, "he was kind of . . . flat."

"He's Church of the Open Bible, for God's sake. Mom goes there because they drive nice cars. Don't ask me how she convinced him to do this river thing. Probably a big check."

They were crossing the pasture field where the cars were parked, and Stu could see people milling around a big table in the back yard.

"Phew," Gloria said. "What's that smell?"

Stu said nothing, but he steered a course through the field so that they passed as far as possible from his truck. When they got close enough to the yard to hear voices, Gloria took the lead. She walked them toward the end of the table where JoAnna stood talking to two men.

"Shouldn't you go change?" Stu asked her.

"I will," she said, "but I want to introduce you to my stepdad first."

Of course. She knew how to act. She was not afraid of these people, not like Stu was. She belonged. She took after her mother in that respect. JoAnna reigned—a queen wherever she was. Stu had admired that about her, at first. He thought being married to her meant he would reign too.

JoAnna and the two men stopped talking and turned toward Stu and Gloria.

"Dad," Gloria said to the taller man with the silver hair, "this is my Dad."

The man smiled.

"That's a fairly confusing introduction," JoAnna said.

The man held out his hand. "Ken Riley," he said.

Stu took the hand, "Stuart Jakes."

"I'm going to change," Gloria said, and then she disappeared into the crowd.

JoAnna introduced the other man, a friend of theirs whose name Stu forgot as soon as it was spoken.

"She sure has grown up," Stu said.

"Hmph," said JoAnna. "Long way to go."

"Popular girl," Ken said. "Big future."

Stu did not nod. Time was when JoAnna thought Stu had a big future, too, and he hated the thought of Gloria suffering through anything like that.

The guy whose name Stu had forgotten asked what Stu did.

"Commercial fishing," Stu said.

"Really?" the guy said, and all three of them smiled as if to say that they had smelled as much.

"I run a line of three hundred crab pots off a thirty-foot boat," Stu said. "Thinking about getting a second boat." It was a lie, of course. He had thought about it, but it was nowhere near possible. "I bring in three hundred bushels of blue gold a week." That was a lie too, twice what he really did. He hated himself. Double what he really did was still a smelly nothing to these people.

JoAnna rolled her eyes, or maybe she just looked at the sky.

Clouds were moving in from the west, and dusk was making its way up the hill.

It would have been polite now to ask Ken and the other guy what they did, but Stu did not want to hear their titles and have to ask what they meant. The guy was looking at him, letting the pause stretch out. JoAnna and Ken were watching too.

"Still trap eels?" JoAnna said at last.

"In season," Stu said.

"Now there's an awful job." JoAnna eyed him, hawk-like. She turned to Ken. "You scoop eels into this barrel that has holes in the bottom to let the water out. Then you lift the barrel and dump the eels into the buyer's tank. But eels make this, like, mucus when they get thrown together, so these long streams of eel snot dangle from the holes in the barrel and it gets all over you." JoAnna turned to Stu. "Remember that kid who worked for you that spring? Remember he brought his girlfriend to watch?"

Stu did not remember.

"Kid finished up and walked toward his girl," JoAnna said, "shirt and pants all shiny with eel snot, and that girl's eyes just went flat. Remember? She got in her car and drove off. Left him standing there—snotty shirt shining in the morning sun."

Stu wanted to tell them what he liked about his work—how he liked being out on the bay in a small boat exposed to whatever the day might serve up. It made him feel—he couldn't explain it—it made him feel alive by the very smallness of what he was. He was only a tiny spark, but because all that emptiness loomed over him, the spark felt bright and warm. He didn't know how to explain it to these people, though—to people who made it their business to push the emptiness away with their money.

No, Stu liked being a waterman, and when JoAnna finally figured that out, the trouble really started. She had not married a waterman. It was not what she had dreamed of. He made a living for them, but it was not a very good living by her standards, and worse yet, he made it, as JoAnna used to say, at the bottom of the food chain.

She had not moved out right away, but when she did, she treated him as if he were some sort of mistake that she could simply erase. It had, as Stu once put it to his lawyer, gutted him.

He took up with a married woman and was glad for a while that somebody noticed his existence. But he had caught the divorce disease from JoAnna, it seemed, because the married woman left her husband and left Stu, too. He had been, she explained, just a part of the problem.

Stu lived like a hermit for a couple years after that, dragging pain through the empty rooms of their trailer. Only when he was stoned or drunk enough did the vacancy in his mind make him feel at home in his abandonment.

"That kid was a pretty sad sack for the rest of the summer," JoAnna was saying. "I don't think he ever did figure out what happened, do you Stu?"

"Sometimes," Stu said, "it doesn't do much good to figure out what has happened to you."

Ken snorted. "Ignorance doesn't do much good either."

Stu said nothing. He was not here for these people. He was here for Gloria. He had seen her come out of the house wearing jeans and earrings and lipstick. One of the boys who had been in the back at the river came up behind her and tugged her hair. She turned around and gave him a killing look, but he only fell back a step and then followed her into the crowd.

"Except maybe for preachers," Ken was saying. "Ignorance seems to be their best friend."

"Tell *her* that," JoAnna said. "Just be thankful I didn't get the preacher she wanted. He would have shouted at us until we'd have been glad to go to hell just to be rid of him."

"I don't think that would have done it," Ken said.

JoAnna smiled, significantly, at Stu. "Where does she get this holy roller stuff?"

No, he did not like these people, and he did not like his ex-wife.

The clouds had spread over the sky, and night had risen out of the river bottom to claim the hill. A few people had already said their goodbyes and were heading to their cars.

Stu saw Gloria talking to an older kid who was tall and good looking. The kid reached into his pocket and drew out a key ring, which he jingled in front of Gloria. She was thrilled. Who knew which car was his, which convertible, which expensive toy? The kid looked like a nice boy, and so, of course, Stu wanted to shake a finger in his face.

It was clear, now, why she had not come back. She was ashamed—of his boots and his missing button, of his old truck and his fishy smell. The whole thing, having him come here on the day of her baptism for his first visitation in four years had seemed like a nice gesture when JoAnna mentioned it over the phone. But he saw now that it had been a trap. It was all arranged to accomplish in Gloria's heart what had not been possible to accomplish in the courts.

Ken and JoAnna excused themselves and set about the business of saying goodbye to guests. Stu stood by the table picking at the shrimp, which could have been fresher. Gloria was nowhere to be seen, nor was the boy with the keys. Voices echoed in the woods—boys ran and hollered through the dark. He listened for Gloria, but he wasn't even sure he would recognize her voice if he heard it. Soon, he would have to go, and he hadn't spent twenty minutes with his daughter. He walked into the field and through the remaining cars, but she was not there. The path to the river led down into the dark, but Stu made his way by following his memory and the smell of bare ground. A breeze seemed to kick up when he got near the water. Stu heard it in the high leaves of the trees, but then he realized that it was the sound of the water rushing around rocks.

He stood on the beach listening. The preacher had pulled a young woman from that river, and the little girl, his little girl, the one he had been kept away from, had been washed away. None of it had worked. He had missed his chance. She was old enough now to care about boys and cars and status. She was old enough to be ashamed of her father, and it was clear to Stu that he could never again be who he once was.

He put a hand in his pocket and felt the driftwood fish. It was going to be her baptism present, though now it seemed foolish. He stood on the little beach and pulled the fish from his pocket. He could not see how the grain flowed gracefully from the head to the tail of the invisible weight in his hand. For an eye, there was a hole. On one side, surrounded by a dark circle that made the fish seem sad. The other side was fresh and lively. He was going to tell her that she could turn the fish around whichever way fit her mood that day. But he saw that it was a silly present—far too young for Gloria, now. He cocked his arm and skipped it into the water.

"What was that?" said a voice, her voice.

"Nothing," he said. "What're you doing?"

"Getting away," she said. "They used to be my friends, but I hate them now."

She was sitting on something at the edge of the water. Boys ran in the woods, crashing through branches and laughing. "Gloria!" they called. "Gloria!"

"God," Gloria said.

"This is my daughter," Stu shouted into the darkness. "Leave us alone."

There was scurrying, a hushed conversation, and then silence. A screech owl called, chilling the dark with its shivering whistle.

Stu sat next to her. In the dark he had thought it was a log, but it was a boat, a wooden row boat. He had seen it at the baptism, its bow pulled well up onto the sand.

"Well," Stu said, "do you feel different?"

"What?"

"Baptized, purified, reborn."

"Oh," she said. "That." She shifted her position. "Know why I did it?"

"To piss your mother off?"

"Maybe."

Stu could hear the smile in her voice.

"I used to come down here to smell the smells and remember how it was when we all lived in that trailer. We used to go boating and everything smelled like mud. I loved it there," she said. "And then Grandma died and Mom and I left and wound up here, and she said you might not even be my dad. Why did she do that? Why does she hate you so bad?"

"I don't know, honey. You'd have to ask her about that. Probably, I wasn't what she wanted me to be."

Gloria grunted. "Who is?"

"Hard to please," Stu said. "Always was."

"Well, I don't even try," Her voice was tight and trembling. "She shouldn't have said that about you because you are my dad. Right?"

"What do *you* think?" he said.

"Bitch." She was crying now. Stu could hear it in her voice. "Fucking bitch."

He put his arm around Gloria and let himself be swept away on wonderful, warm tears.

Gloria sniffed and raised her head. "There's no mud here," she said, "and the fishing's no good, and there's no boating."

Stu patted what they sat on. "Somebody boats."

"You can't row against the current," Gloria said. "A guy Mom knows brings a motor sometimes."

From deep in the darkness of the woods came a call: "Glo-rie, Glo-rie . . ."

"Let's go," Gloria said.

But Stu didn't want to go back. Didn't want to get in his truck and have only these few minutes to think about during the long drive home.

"Not yet."

"Come on," she said, and she swung her legs into the boat. "Shove us off."

It was like all the childish games he used to play with her—foolish games where you start something you know you can't finish just to see what will happen. He got up and stood at the bow of the boat. Around him, the darkness was impenetrable. It was like being on the bay in bad weather—just himself, and now Gloria, against the emptiness. He shoved off, and by the time he hopped in and got the oars in his hands, the boat had turned a slow circle and the current caught it. He couldn't see a thing. The sky, the trees, the river, the shore—everything was a uniform blackness. Stu felt his stomach roll and his head spin.

"Whoa," Gloria said. "Which way are we?"

On either side there was the sound of rushing water where rocks and fallen trees broke the river into trouble. Instinct told him to move toward the sounds, since that was where the river made itself known. But he fought the urge and steered instead toward the quiet places where it seemed there was nothing. His guts fought the idea, but his brain won. Smooth, clear water was silent, and so he bit back the fear and pointed the boat toward nothingness. It raised the hair on his arms, this faith, this knowledge, and Stu had that old, small feeling of safety in the midst of danger, a feeling that was all the brighter for the darkness which pressed in so closely.

"This is scary," Gloria said.

There was so much he wanted to tell her. He loved her; he cared about her. He hadn't wanted to disappear for all those years, but he had been confused and lost, and now he was sorry.

Gloria scrambled up into the bow. "I don't like this," she said.

He wanted to tell her that he would not be able to be a real father, not the kind who could protect her from trouble, not somebody who could catch her up in his arms at the first sign of danger. No, he would have to leave soon, and most of the time he'd be far away. Most of the time he would just be a part of the huge emptiness around her. He didn't know how to say it though, and he was afraid of sounding like some sort of spook who breaks through to the world with so much to say that it comes out like desperate and terrifying gibberish.

"God," Gloria said. "I think I'm dizzy."

"It gives you the chills, doesn't it?" Stu said.

"No," she said.

The noise of rushing water pressed in on either side, but the darkness pulled them toward silence. Stu felt himself expanding as if the edges between him and all that was not him were dissolving in the dark.

"Okay," Gloria said. "That's enough. I want to go back."

Stu listened for a silent place near shore, a place where smooth water might reach right up to the river bank. He told Gloria to be patient, or at least he thought he told her, but he couldn't be sure that he hadn't just imagined saying it, or that it hadn't come out sounding like the water rushing around fallen trees.

"I won't be able to see you very often, honey, but I love you. You know?"

"Daddy," she said. "Please. I want to go back."

He could feel her up there on the bow, straining toward shore, so he worked the oars and angled the boat toward the bank—toward the life she would have to live without him—family, friends, the dumb and dirty boys. Soon, they were among the rocks and the tangled roots and the familiar sounds of troubled water again. The bow bumped and scraped and then struck sand. Stu used the oars to hold the boat on the bank while Gloria climbed out. He felt like a ferryman delivering a precious passenger. He could tell that she had grabbed the bow line and was steadying the boat for him. But he didn't want to get out. He didn't want to contract again into himself, into his truck, into his life alone back home. He wanted to back the boat off the bank and disappear into the night, into the emptiness, so that he could always be there for her when she needed him.

Waiting
Room

The freezer was already half full of dilemmas, but Stu curled the calico cat into a plastic bag and laid it next to the ice trays anyway. When it dragged its sick self to the front steps three days ago, Stu could not decide whether to shoot it or take it to the vet. It died before he made up his mind, but then Stu could not decide whether to bury it or throw it in the trash. Thank goodness for the freezer. Already, there was a stack of credit card offers, a grey plastic box containing his mother's ashes, and a pair of moldy baby shoes stuffed in next to the frozen orange juice. But there was still plenty of room for the cat, and, Stu supposed, plenty more after that.

When she called to ask if she could come to his place for the procedure, Stu did not know what to say. She was not yet seventeen and would have to drive across the state on a learner's permit. No, he said, it was not a good idea.

But she was desperate, she told him. She needed his help, and she needed to be where they had all lived before the divorce tore everything apart. It would be the first time in seven years that Gloria had come to his place, their place.

"Well . . ." he said.

"Well?" she said.

"Well, I don't know."

"I'm coming," she said. Then she told him when.

"Okay," he said. "I guess. I'll be here."

"You guess you'll be there, or you guess it's okay?"

He could hear a hum in the phone line.

"Dad!" Gloria said.

"Yes," he had said. "I'll be here. I will."

And so now he sat on a kitchen chair that he brought out onto the little porch where the cat had decided to die—a cat that hadn't wanted a single thing to do with Stu until the end. He leaned the chair back on two legs and looked up the sandy drive toward the road. The oaks were beginning to show the red that came upon them before they would go brown.

A car turned into the drive. It looked new and expensive. Stu lowered the chair and leaned forward. But the car stopped. Then it backed up and drove off in the direction it had come.

Stu's mother used to say that when you didn't know what to do, well then, you probably shouldn't do much at all. But it was harder to do nothing than it seemed. He closed his eyes there on the porch and decided to sit in the fall sun and not wait.

It was the slow season at Pressy's. Stu had finished eeling two weeks ago, and the crabs were gone for the year. The other parts of his job—running Pressy's sand dredge and worming parts at the junkyard slowed down in the fall, too. But it was more complicated this year. Pressy was down with emphysema, and the office at the yard was dark most days. Stu kept up his old routines though: it wasn't quite like doing nothing, but it was close.

The car was back, and this time it did not stop and turn around but came all the way down and pulled into the parking spot by the trailer. The door opened, and Gloria got out. She was harried by her first long drive alone, and, Stu could tell, short of sleep. Her eyelids drooped and her mouth hung open a little.

"It didn't look like the right place," she said.

Stu stood up. "Trees are bigger."

"Maybe," she said, "but everything seems small."

He stepped off the porch and took the travel bag from her. She hugged him. "Want to sit in the sun?" he said. "I could bring out another chair."

"Maybe later," she said. "But first I want to see it all. I want to see everything."

He opened the front door and let her into the trailer.

Gloria took two steps in and stopped. She scanned the living room and the kitchen. Stu could not remember the last time anyone had been in his house. He had picked up his clutter and even dusted and vacuumed. Still, the place was tired. The furniture dated from the days when his ex-wife had tried to liven the place up.

"I remember that window." Gloria crossed the room and knelt on the couch. She folded her arms on the back and peered out at the reeds and the dock and the bow of 247. "The river was wider back then," Gloria said, "and was that dump always there?"

"It's not a dump, honey. It's a salvage yard. I work there. You and I spent lots of time wandering around that place."

"That's it?" she said. "I remember. I just don't remember it being so . . . close." She turned around and sat on the couch. Her eyes roamed the kitchen and then fastened on the hall. "Can I see my room? I mean what used to be my room."

"It's still yours, honey."

He opened the door to the tiny room, and Gloria went in. There was a dresser and a twin bed. Gloria's posters and drawings from third or fourth grade still hung on the wall.

Her hands went to her mouth. "Oh, Bahbie," she said.

Stu had found the stuffed rabbit under her bed. He had knocked years of dust off it and put it on her pillow.

She picked it up and twisted the key in its back. Stu remembered the plinky melody. Gloria hugged Bahbie and sat on the bed.

Stu sat next to her and put his arm around her shoulders.

"Mom said she didn't know what happened to you," Gloria said. "Lost in the move. Oh, I missed you."

"Found it under the bed," Stu said.

"All these years just waiting for me."

"Pretty patient."

Gloria put the rabbit back on the pillow. "You stay here," she said to it. "I'll sleep with you tonight."

Stu opened the window, and the breeze came in off the marshes.

"That smell," Gloria said, inhaling the methane-y air. "It's awful, and I love it."

Stu brought Gloria's bag into the room. "Do you want to take a rest?" Stu said. "I'll make us some dinner in a while."

"What are we having?"

"Spaghetti? Salad?"

That was fine. Gloria lay on the bed and curled her arm around Bahbie.

Stu closed the door. It was strange—someone else in the house. He filled a pot with water, and while it warmed, he made a salad of lettuce and carrots. Then he put sauce in a pan and turned the burner on low. Dinner could be on the table in fifteen minutes, but maybe he should let her rest longer. He turned the burner down and decided to give her half an hour. But maybe that was too long. No. He couldn't decide, so he had a little rum. Coke for color, the clink of ice in the glass, and yes, it was warm like home.

He went out onto the porch and was just ready to sit and watch the evening when he realized that the glass was already empty. Another quick mix and he was ready for the sun to sink out of sight.

It took one more rum for the glow to disappear, but Gloria was still not up. Stu put more water in the pot. He turned up the heat on the sauce and then checked on the girl again. She was curled up, just the way she used to sleep. When he touched her shoulder she grumbled, so he decided to let her stay. He could go ahead and make dinner. Maybe the smell would wake her, and if not, well, spaghetti kept.

He was washing his plate when Gloria stumbled from the bedroom, her hair tousled and her eyes puffy. "Slept too long," she said.

"Didn't know if I should wake you."

"Couldn't tell where I was," she said, "or who. Just sat there in the dark waiting to be. Then I smelled the swamps, and it all came back."

Stu fixed her a plate, and she sat at the table and picked at the food. "Is it okay?"

"Oh sure," she said, "I'm just tired."

He fixed himself another drink at the sink and sat down across from her. She took little bites and watched him as she chewed. She nodded at his glass. "Is this what you do at night?"

He was not used to scrutiny. Rum never seemed to have opinions about what he should or shouldn't do.

"Is that why she left you?"

"You'd have to ask her," he said. "I didn't drink much back then. No, I was Mr. Oops."

"Well," Gloria said, "like father like daughter. Steppie says I navigate via mistake."

"That's how we all do, honey." Accidents ran the universe, as far as Stu could tell. People bounced from error to bad luck and back again while God gave the "who knew?" shrug.

"If it wasn't for me, you two wouldn't have gotten married, and then you wouldn't have divorced, and I wouldn't be Glory-Oops."

"It wasn't you," Stu said.

"Hmm?"

"We got married because your mother was pregnant, but it wasn't with you. Your mom had a miscarriage."

Gloria sat back and looked at the ceiling.

"That was the one we married for."

Gloria looked at her plate. She put her fork down.

"A few months later, all Mom wanted was to get pregnant again. And that was you, fixing what had been wrong. A regular blessing."

She leaned forward. "Boy or girl?"

"Huh?"

"The one I made up for."

"Oh, I don't know, honey. Never had the nerve to ask your mother."

"God," Gloria said.

"Yeah."

"Everything is so fucked up."

Stu hunched his shoulders.

"No," Gloria said. "You don't just shake your head and go on. It hurts too bad."

"I know."

"No, you don't." Gloria was glaring at him. "What you do is drink."

"Look," he said. But he didn't know what to say next.

"What's the point?"

"Of?"

"Of living," Gloria said.

"Oh man," Stu said. "You've got to live. Why look for a reason?"

"No, you don't," Gloria said. "You don't have to live, and you don't have to have babies, either."

Well, they were right in the middle of the minefield now, and Stu was drunk. "People love you, Glorie."

"My family?" she said. "My fucked up family?"

"Look, you can't go back in time," he said. "Family is family, even if it's not perfect."

"Oh, but you *can* go back in time," Gloria said. "You know what Steppie says? He says an abortion is not like killing something, it's more like pruning a bush. Cut it back a little and she'll fill in even better than before. That's what he says. I should just have a season cut out of me, like the summer never happened."

Stu wanted to go out onto the porch and stare at the night until rum brought the curtain down and he could sleep.

"If you had it to do over again," Gloria said, "what would you do?"
"About?"

"About having a kid."

"I don't know, honey." he said

"Mom said that the boy she really loved didn't love her back," Gloria said. "She married you because she was pregnant and desperate. But she still loved that other guy."

Stu nodded. It occurred to him that JoAnna might not have been merely hateful when she claimed he was not Gloria's father. She might have been clinging to a dream.

"It was a mistake," Gloria said. "Your marriage was a mistake, and I was a mistake, and that first baby was a mistake, too."

"Aren't we all?" Stu said.

"Does that help?" Gloria said. "Do you think you're helping me?"

Stu didn't know. He was just saying what came into his head. "Maybe it's late," he said. "Maybe we should go to bed."

"Maybe you can sleep."

"Maybe," Stu said. He got up from the table and said good night.

"Right," Gloria said, "real good."

It turned out that Stu was the one who was not able to sleep. He should not have told her about that first baby. He should have let his daughter believe that if she had been aborted the world would have been a better, happier place, not that it would have been, but allowing her to think so would have made it easier for her, now, to do what she had decided to do. Stu groaned and rolled over a hundred times. How could he let her think that she was anything but a blessing? He wanted to crawl out of bed and into the freezer.

Gloria came out of her room shortly after eight. She was wearing a tee shirt and shorts. "I knew where I was this time," she said. "I just didn't know when. Bahbie in my arms, those posters on the wall. I was a kid again. I know that kid, but she doesn't know me. Doesn't know how much trouble I've gotten myself into."

She was not supposed to eat any breakfast, so Stu had a bowl of cereal alone, while Gloria walked outside by the creek.

At nine, he tried to start his truck, but they had to take her car instead. The clinic was in a building that might have been insurance offices. The receptionist pointed them to the waiting room and said that the counselor would be with them shortly.

Two couples and one lone woman sat in the chairs. One couple looked married. They had matching thousand-yard stares and seemed somehow sealed up together. The other couple was a terrified girl and a huge boy. They held hands, their interlocked fingers white. Only the lone woman made real eye contact, and there was a kind of warning in that look. It was not like other waiting rooms Stu had known, where some coughed, some limped, some moaned. Here the complaint was always the same—not enough love to meet demand, not enough hope to keep the doubts at bay.

The counselor came in a few minutes and took them to a small room. She explained the procedure and the law and showed Stu where to sign the permission forms.

He clicked the pen and leaned over. For the first time in years, he felt like a parent again. Gloria needed him—his permission. His daughter's happiness, her success, was in his hands. Suddenly, now that it was too late, he wanted to ask questions. Did she love the boy? But he knew the answers wouldn't matter. She was too young. Just as her mother had been too young. The ink trailed out behind the tip of the pen. Stu had the feeling that he was not writing but erasing—protecting his daughter from the very conditions that had created her.

He stopped after the "Stu," unsure where to go next. He would have liked to put the form in the freezer.

"Why me?" he whispered to her.

"Mom runs everything," Gloria said. "But not this. Not now."

Stu finished the forms and gave them to the counselor. "Questions?" she said.

Gloria looked at Stu. When he shook his head, her eyes narrowed. "No," she told the woman.

In pre-op, everything was white—the walls, the uniforms. There were no pictures, no windows. Speakers in the ceiling murmured indecipherable pages over muted musak. It made for a dream-like laziness, inhuman and unreal. Nurses took over, closing the curtain while they dressed Gloria in a gown and started an I.V. They put her on a gurney and told Stu he would have to go to the recovery waiting room.

The hallway seemed to stretch forever; its walls were lined with doors to operating suites. At the end, just before the exit, was the sign for the recovery waiting room. Stu settled in with the huge boy and the husband to wait for the world to begin again.

In an hour, a nurse told Stu he could see Gloria. She was in a post-op recovery room—eight beds separated by white curtains. He did not recognize the other forms he glimpsed in the beds except for the lone woman, whose hands twitched nervously. Gloria smiled wanly when he stepped through her curtain. She was ashen and groggy. Her speech was thick and she kept forgetting what time it was. Stu pulled up a chair and held her hand. After an hour, she was more like herself. When he asked how she felt, she said, "Done." Before the next hour passed, she was dressed and sitting in a chair. They got a sheet of instructions from the nurse, and Stu held Gloria's arm and walked her toward the exit, which opened on a side street far from the clinic's entrance. They were supposed to focus on the future now, on the new start they had given themselves.

The sun hurt, and a cold wind had come up. Stu hugged Gloria close, and they made their way to the car.

"Look how blue the sky is," Gloria said. She did not seem upset. Perhaps it was the drugs. She just seemed empty.

At home, Stu fixed her a place on the couch. He got her something to drink and made toast and jam. He sat there with her feet in his lap while she napped. Stu watched soap operas. All those goings on. No matter how bad things were, a soap opera could make you feel lucky. In the evening, they ordered pizza, and Gloria felt well enough to eat it on the porch with a blanket around her.

Stu had taken a few slugs of rum in the afternoon, but in the evening, he made a show of putting mostly coke in the glass.

A warm front came through, and the cloud bank made for a spectacular sunset. The air grew warmer as night descended around them, and they stayed on the porch smelling the smells and watching the stars reclaim the sky.

Gloria got up and wobbled into the bathroom. He heard the toilet flush. The sounds of Gloria fixing herself something to drink in the kitchen came to him from far away. JoAnna had told him once that she thought being in the womb was like swinging in a hammock on a hot, hot day. You drifted there, only half awake and you could reach everything in your world. Everything was right there. Yes. Rum made him feel that way. It brought the edges in close, wrapped a little world tightly around him so that nothing was a mystery.

The screen door slammed, and Stu heard Gloria settle into her chair. "What are you doing?" she said.

"Hmm?" he said. "Just feeling the night."

She leaned toward him, then, forcing her face into his vision. "I mean what are you doing with your life? A trailer by the dump? A stinking swamp?"

No. Pressy would set him up running the yard when the time came. And that time was near. Stu would never get rich, but he could get a better house and let some of his other chores go. He was moving. He had a future.

"Why is there a dead cat in the freezer?" Gloria said.

Stu rose inside himself, up though the rummy haze, to peer out of his eyes.

Gloria was leaning back in her chair staring at him with her chin in her hand.

"It was just a half-wild cat," he said. "But I didn't want to throw it away. So I'll just wait until I know what's right."

"Jesus Christ, Dad, so you put it in the freezer? Just bury it. It doesn't hurt to treat things better than they deserve, you know. It's just too freaky. What's wrong with you?

He wondered if it was a fair question.

"God," Gloria said, "tell me that I am not going to wind up a divorced drunk living by the dump and freezing the cats."

Stu closed his eyes. He should have helped her do this thing. He should have helped her look forward, helped her be optimistic so he could share hope with her now. But he had done nothing, or as close to it as he had been able. What had he been thinking? "I couldn't decide," he said. "It was just a half-wild cat"

"Go to bed, Dad. Sleep it off."

He wanted to tell her not to talk to him that way. Somebody needed to give her rules, but Stu had no idea what rules those might be. He rose stiffly from his chair and gave her a look, part anger, part hurt. He went in to bed, where again, he did not sleep, but just wandered among regrets, groaning each time he turned over. Toward dawn, he finally drifted off, and when he woke, the sun was streaming in the window.

Gloria was up and packed. She was sitting at the kitchen table sipping a cup of coffee. She seemed much older, much more in control than she had. Her clothes were expensive, her make-up was perfect, her hair was cut, he now noticed, just so. She did not belong at that battered table in his shabby trailer. Hers was a different world altogether, and he understood, now, why she had wanted him to help her with the abortion. His was a place where she could dump unpleasant memories.

He had a cup of coffee with her, and then she got into the car and left. It all seemed like a dream, and he remembered now that he had dreamed this morning that the aborted kid was Gloria, gone forever.

In her room, he held the sheets to his nose. He wanted Bahbie. He wanted to feel the rabbit's yellow fur and hear the music box's old tune. He wanted tears, wanted to feel something even though it was pain. But Bahbie was nowhere to be found, not on the shelves and not in the drawers. The only sign that Gloria had been in the room at all was a small dark box she had left on her pillow. Wisps of white stuffing clung to it, and a winding key protruded from one side. Stu knew immediately what it was. It belonged in the freezer, but he could not bring himself to touch it.

Daddies
Don't Care

S tu was pumping fuel into 247 while Karen was in the marina
store buying Pampers and flirting with the clerk. He could
see her in there beyond the Lottery and Coors Light signs. She shifted
her one-year-old from hip to hip, throwing a little extra action into
the process, and when the child's hand came to rest on her breast,
Karen just smiled at the clerk and let his eyes go wherever they chose.

What did she think? Some strange boy was going to take an inter-
est in her even with a kid? What went on in her head? Stu wanted to
know. He ought to turn off the pump right then and walk in there.
Ought to grab her arm and tell her that they were still far too close.

She came out of the store a minute later, all nipples and smiles, and
walked down the dock toward 247. "They've got showers and washing machines!" she said. Her eyes were brighter than Stu had seen
them since she ran out of crank two days earlier. The boat rocked
when she stepped onboard. "And diapers," she said.

She set the kid down on the deck and tried to help her stand, but
as soon as she lifted that last finger, the kid plopped down hard on her
rear end. Karen made her mouth into an "oh" and clapped her hands
beneath her chin. She looked toward Stu.

"We're far enough away, right? We could stay here."

Stu wasn't sure who "we" were, if it included him or not. "It's only
one county away," he told her.

She straightened up and scanned the dock.

Two old men sat on a bench outside the store. The skinny one
almost disappeared behind the pile of knuckles on top of his cane.

The other guy had a long nose over a little mouth, like an exclamation point. The piney hill rose beyond them, with its cabins, fire pits, and picnic tables.

Karen wiped hair from the side of her face. "It seems further," she said.

For three days, they had powered up the winding river, through tidal swamps and endless reeds, and all along the way, she had found place after place where she wanted to stop and get off: a kudzu-covered junk yard, a tiny island with one dwarf hickory, and innumerable muddy landings where muskrat trappers and duck hunters launched their john boats. They were all impossible, of course. Stu had kept going, powering through endless twists and turns that transformed a single mile into seven.

At night, they anchored. They cooked in the tiny cabin, crouching around like trolls. And they slept in the V-berth, though it took days for Karen to come down far enough to sleep.

On the third day, they had passed the tide line. The river narrowed, and trees crowded the banks. The water was fresh, and everything smelled sweet. Karen seemed to think they were in another world altogether. "Any place along in here would do just fine," she kept telling him. But Stu kept the bow pointed into the current and set the throttle so the diesel was happy.

Then in the middle of the afternoon, she was sitting in the mate's seat, exhausted but frazzled, with the kid dangling from her lap. The woods up ahead darkened as if there was a wall of weather up there. Stu put 247 in neutral. The boat coasted, gradually slowing against the current. The trees parted overhead, and the sun shined down as they drifted into the basin at the foot of a dam.

Karen sat up and squinted.

Algae-stained stone twenty feet tall made a wall in the woods, a wall across the river. From its top, a veil of water fell and made rainbows.

"Unh," she said.

Stu had agreed to get her out of there, out of that town where bikers and cops were fighting over the scraps of Karen.

"It's okay," he said.

The siren blared, and two giant doors, tall as the dam itself, slowly swung open. A cabin cruiser emerged and powered past them toward salt water.

Lights at the lock turned green and Stu put 247 in gear.

Karen pressed her foot against the deck as if there might be a brake there.

The air filled with mist as they got closer to the lock. The rainbows disappeared, and huge stone blocks rose on either side. 247 slipped between walls, dark with algae, and stopped at the closed doors on the other end of the lock. Water leaked from the joints and poured over the giant rivets and huge hinges. Stu tied off to the lock rings and shut the diesel down. Slowly, the doors behind them closed. Water dripping from the walls echoed in the giant tomb.

Karen could not seem to catch her breath. She kept her eyes on the small square of sky above them, and gulped air like a fish. Her grip on the kid loosened and the girl lay there in her lap, corpsey in that way she had.

247 shied in the upwelling that roiled beneath them as the lock began to fill. If it hadn't been for the kid, Stu would never have gotten involved. Karen was not his problem, but she had come to the Basin in the middle of the night three days ago and thrust the kid at Stu and said, "I *got* her!"

Fine white hair fanned out around the kid's head. She had on pajamas with feet and she held a small stuffed elephant in one hand. At the sight of Stu. she had gone stiff and dropped the animal into the boat.

"Babysitter was asleep," Karen had said, "and I *got* her."

Even in the weak light of the Basin, he had seen that Karen's eyes were glazed, wide, speeding eyes. Clearly trouble. Everybody at the marina knew she was divorcing an ex-detective and trading for protection and crank from the bikers across the river. As soon as she got on board, Stu heard someone step onto the floating dock at the far end of the marina. The couplings between sections rattled and the sound followed whoever it was like the clatter of a metal wave.

Karen did not turn toward it. Her speeding ears were all-hearing. Her speeding mind all-knowing. "That's him," she had said. "Let me in."

Stu said nothing. He had been asleep. It was late.

"At least let me hide her."

Stu narrowed his eyes.

"She'll stay quiet," Karen assured him. "She's used to—you know, little places—drawers, cupboards."

Stu stared at her.

"Her father," Karen said. "You'd have to know the son of a bitch."

Stu climbed out on the deck and led Karen forward. He lifted a hatch and they both looked down at the big Danforth anchor and the two hundred feet of mud-stained line. Karen knelt and bunched the line into a sort of bed. She set the girl in the middle, and nestled the elephant in her arms. The girl squeezed the animal and rolled onto her side, drawing her knees toward her chin.

Karen stood. "It's okay," she said. "She's used to it."

Stu nodded, but Karen had to push his hand off the hatch and close it herself.

She led him back to the cabin and took off her tee shirt and jeans. Then she crawled into his berth.

They were canned up inside the tiny cabin. Stu squatted on the floor listening to the metal wave come closer and closer until it stopped. The boat rocked. Then the hatch above his head opened just a crack. The man's face seemed huge, filling the gap like that. His nose wrinkled, and he startled when he saw Stu looking back at him.

He wanted to know where Jennifer was.

It was good to have a name for the kid, Stu thought. Without names, things slipped into you, things got to you.

From the berth, Karen's words were slurred as if she was drunk. "Wha?"

"Goddamn it," the guy said. He swung the hatch all the way opened and started to come in, but there was no room for another person. Stu stood up the only way he could—with his head out the hatch. The guy turned away. "Jesus God," he said. "How can you stand it in there?"

Stu knew there was that dead fish and diesel smell all workboats had. He supposed there was also the smell of fried food and the kerosene stove. And there was the smell of Stu, too, perhaps not always so clean.

"Where's Jenn'fer?" Karen said.

The guy glared at her. "Why don't you tell me?"

"How'm I supposed t'know?" She swung her legs out and sat on the edge of the berth, topless in her panties. "I been ri' here."

"Seriously?" he said. "How old is he, Karen? Take a look. Take a whiff. What're you doing?"

"Takes care me," Karen said, sweetly drunk.

"We don't want trouble," Stu heard himself say.

The guy barked out a laugh. "Listen, pal," he said, "if you got her on your boat, take it from me, you got trouble."

"Where's she?" Karen said.

The guy said nothing.

"I gotta fin' her!" Karen stumbled out of Stu's berth, but she plowed into the stove and wound up on the floor by Stu's feet.

"You drunk whore," the guy said. "How'd I ever wind up with you?"

"Nothing better happen to her. Son of a bitch!" Karen cried, pretend-drunk and hysterical there on the cabin floor. "Oh, God," she said. "What did you *do?*"

The guy winced.

"You better find her, you prick. Lost her? Jesus Christ. What did you do?"

Stu watched the guy—a divorcing man forced to listen again to a voice he hated. It was too much. The guy set his jaw and gave Stu a look. Then he was gone. They listened to him clattering away down the dock.

"He'll be back," Stu said.

Karen shook her head and wrinkled her nose the same way the guy had.

As soon as he was gone, they went up front and knelt by the locker. Karen opened the hatch and the girl lay there, motionless as a mummy in a tangle of muddy line. Karen lifted the thing and pressed it to her chest. There was no movement, no sound. The girl's mouth hung open.

Stu couldn't breathe. The elephant was caught beneath coils of line. He wanted to scream, wanted to tear down the sky. He wanted to call the kid's name, but he could not remember what it was already.

And so it was anybody, even his own daughter, even the child she had been carrying.

Karen cooed and soothed, praying, it seemed, over a corpse. But the girl stirred and cried tired sobs into her mother's chest.

Stu thought it was the most beautiful thing he had ever heard.

She would never remember that anchor locker. But the smell of sea-rot and mud, the terrifying safety of darkness—who knows how many things would take root in a kid?

As the lock doors swung open, the reservoir slowly grew before them. Ten miles of water, like a beam, sparkled in the sun. Stu started the diesel and powered out of the lock. They could see the marina, with its store and its fuel dock and its campground in the pines. Then it turned out that they had showers and washers and it was like heaven to Karen—a different world and far enough away from her old one to seem safe.

Stu shut off the fuel pump. He left the nozzle in the deck port and took Karen by the elbow outside the store. He tried to walk her away from the bench where Knuckles and Surprise sat, but she refused to budge.

They were only a forty-five-minute trip by car from where they had started, he told her. Maybe it felt safe, but they were still too close for it to *be* safe.

Karen turned toward Knuckles and smiled her prettiest. She was young, and her looks were not yet completely ruined by the speed.

The old man nodded. "Safe as can be," he said. "Cops come through two, three times a night."

Karen carried the kid over to the bench and set her down on her feet. She tried to get her to stand, but the baby kept plopping down on her behind. Karen bent over, in her skimpy top, and stood her up again.

She asked the geezers where their boats were, where they lived, how far it was to town, who owned the marina, and what they knew about the boy who clerked in the store.

They knew everything, of course, and told it all to her. Stu thought that they would have given her their bank account numbers, too, if she had just kept bending over to stand that kid up.

He finished filling the tanks and closed the deck-caps. The total on the pump read $283.

Karen dug into the waist of her shorts and pulled out six fifties. Knuckles raised a bushy eyebrow when she handed them to Stu.

After he paid, Stu came out of the store. He took Karen by the elbow, and she picked up the kid. He walked them back to the boat. They went below and she put the kid down on the berth and turned toward Stu.

He tried to catch her eyes, but she bowed beneath the low ceiling and would not look at him.

"Maybe," he said, "if you took ten dollars this would be far enough, but you took a kid, for God's sake. So no. No way this is far enough." They had to keep going. "It's his daughter," Stu said. "He'll come for her."

Karen shook her head at the floor. Then she wriggled out of her halter top and stepped out of her shorts.

Stu went out to stand on the work deck. "There's another marina," he said. It was thirty miles farther at the head of the reservoir. JoAnna lived not too far beyond it with her second husband. Near them lived Stu's daughter and the son-in-law Stu had never really met. And his grandkid, whose name Stu did not know.

Karen pulled the baby's dress over her head and took off her diaper. Everything went into the pile of laundry.

Jennifer, he thought. That was her name. "It's two more counties away," Stu said.

"I'm not worried," Karen said. "Daddies don't care that much."

She put on a bikini she produced from her bag. Then, laundry in one arm and naked kid in the other, she crouched out of the cabin.

He spoke slowly to her. "He *will* keep coming."

Karen turned and faced Stu. "He seen me," she said, and she opened her hands in a way that took in Stu and his boat. Then she stepped onto the dock and walked past Knuckles and Surprise to the store. He could see her in there, nearly naked, leaning over the counter buying detergent and getting quarters for the washing machine. The clerk smiled at something she said and took a long time making change. She disappeared into another room then, where, Stu supposed, the washers and dryers and showers were.

Stu's mother used to say waiting was prayer and that if you were patient, time would fill like a womb. Stu used the dock hose to fill 247's water tank, and when Karen had still not returned, he killed time by shooting water at the scum line on the hull. There had never been much point in washing the boat back home. Each day brought more stinking bait, more fish, more waste. Only the work-deck got brushed and hosed to keep it from being slippery. He picked up the brush now and took a swipe at the hull. It left a white streak.

He took a few more until a section of 247 was white, and then he could not stop because it was so evident now that the boat was filthy. He scrubbed the hull all around. Then he dragged the hose on board and sprayed water into the bilges. He flipped a switch and pumped it all out again. He did this over and over, until much of the diesel and dead fish smell had been dumped overboard where it made a rainbow slick in the water. Stu sat in the captain's seat and watched the sheen dissipate.

Then he went forward and blasted the anchor locker with the hose, washing mud and salt down the drain hole. He pulled out all the line and scrubbed it with the brush. Then he washed the sides and the bottom of the locker until they were almost white again. He wanted to get a kid out of there, out of his memory.

Down below, the boat smelled fresh. He rooted through his canned food. The humidity on 247 had peeled away most of the labels, so meals for Stu were often a gamble. The first can he opened was yams. He dumped them in a pan and put them on the stove to warm.

Karen came from the store, her hair turbaned in a towel. He saw her standing by the bench. She had a bundle of clean clothes in one arm, and the kid, wearing a Pampers, in the other.

Knuckles stumbled up off the bench to help. She gave him the laundry and put both arms around the kid. They came down the dock, a strange trio, Stu thought. Grandfather, granddaughter, and great granddaughter, maybe.

Knuckles dumped the laundry into Stu's arms, and Karen thanked him. She sniffed as she entered the cabin, then she took a deep breath.

Her laundry went onto the berth, and she sat the kid in the middle. The baby leaned toward food. She wanted, wanted.

"I rented a cabin," Karen said.

*   *   *

In the back room of the store, Stu took off his clothes and lay them on the floor of the shower stall. He turned the water on and lathered up. He used his feet to work soap into his clothes. When the water backed up around his ankles like Stu soup, he turned the shower off and stomped around on his clothes for a while. Then he moved them away from the drain and watched the water swirl away. He turned the water on again until everything was rinsed. He put on dry clothes and walked back to the boat, which seemed to shine there by the dock. He spread his wet clothes on the railings to dry in the evening sun.

The cabin smelled of yams. Karen was folding her little pile of laundry and stuffing it into a bag. She had brushed her hair in a pony-tail, and the little girl was in a dress.

Stu stirred the yams, and the little girl leaned toward him, making the grabby motion.

Stu cooled a spoon-tip and offered it.

She liked yams.

"She's hungry," Stu said.

Karen shrugged.

The kid still had a mouthful when Karen lifted her from the berth and pulled the bag onto her shoulder.

Stu filled the hatchway. "Let her eat," he said.

Karen sat.

He gave her the spoon and stepped out into the cockpit while she fed the girl.

He wasn't sure what he was going to do. His mother's advice would have been to do nothing if you didn't know what to do. But it wasn't a matter of doing nothing. It was a matter of doing something, some particular thing. Some right thing.

He went to the back of the boat and untied the stern line. Then, quietly, he headed to the front, unlaid the figure eight, and dropped the line. The breeze barely moved them at first. In a relaxed, natural way, he walked back to the captain's seat and watched the air take them slowly away from the dock. He would ferry them thirty more miles to the head of the reservoir and leave her there if that was what she wanted, but,they couldn't stay here.

Karen came from the cabin, bag over her shoulder, kid on her hip. She stepped onto the gunwale, and the boat rocked. She hesitated; the gap between dock and boat was already wide.

Stu pressed the button, and a cloud of smoke shot from the stack.

Karen crouched.

"It's too far," Stu said.

She waited for the boat to rock upward, and then she giant stepped with that child in her arms across the gap and onto the dock.

"He'll find you," Stu said.

She looked down at him. "Don't," she said, "try to God me."

"He will."

"He'd have to love us," she said.

So Stu saw how it was. She was not done with her marriage. She wanted to be found, to be brought home.

Stu put 247 in gear and moved away from the dock.

He supposed he could head east and go back home where whatever was washed away on one tide was washed back on the next, salted and pickled, so to speak. The messes went back and forth on the tides until they broke down and settled into the mud, the black ooze, which stank of methane made of everything that ever was.

He shifted into neutral and turned toward the dock to say goodbye, but no one was there.

He had wanted that kid out of his memory. It was Jennifer, and she was gone now.

He put the boat back in gear and throttled up. A puff of dark smoke blew from the stack until the diesel settled in.

He didn't turn back toward the lock and he didn't turn west toward the notch in the horizon either. Getting to the head of the reservoir could take days, and picking his way around sandbars and snags all the way up river would be slow going. It could take weeks to get to the hills where what was left of his own little family had named a kid.

247 churned in circles under the evening sun while Stu waited for time to fill.

Gandy

From his lawn chair on the deck of 247, Stu could see over the bank of the river and into the forest. The shade was deep, and a path led into the trees. Stu traced it with his eyes, moving upward until it rose into the leaves and he lost the way.

A whippoorwill whippoorwilled.

The Green River was a tunnel through the trees, a worm's tube, barely big enough for 247, which was too long now to turn around. Its exhaust stack reached the limbs that arced overhead and the boat sat on the sandy bottom like a little house with ropes drooping to trees on the bank.

Leaning back with his hands behind his head, Stu listened. The shade was deep and peaceful.

Her bare feet showed first among the laurel leaves. Then came her long legs, tan shorts, white shirt—Gloria descending. She had the boy's hand in hers. He was four and he stumbled along beside her, more intent on 247 than the path.

At the bottom of the hill, she tried to direct him to the river, but the boy yanked his hand from hers and squatted there on the path, fingers fumbling with his lips.

Gloria turned her back on him. She stepped to the bank and frowned down at Stu.

He had wanted to make a good impression. He fought the river for a month to get there. It was a testimony, he thought. But Gloria had rolled her eyes when she got her first glimpse of it—a thirty-foot crabbing boat longer than the river was wide sitting awkwardly on the sandy bottom. She had looked down from the bank that first day. "What's this," she said, "your portable wreck?"

Stu put his hands in his lap and smiled up at her. "How's my young man?" he said.

The kid perked up.

"What should we do today?" Stu said.

The boy's fingers stopped moving and formed a sort of grill in front of his mouth. "Fissshh," he said.

Gloria stared at the boy.

He was silent.

"You were four," Stu said, "before you had a word in your head."

Gloria turned to Stu and forced out a breath. "Don't," she hissed, "make him play favorites."

"My favorite grandson." Stu smiled and winked at the boy.

"Your only," Gloria said.

The boy came to the bank. He had dark hair and a long neck like his mother. Stu reached up and helped him into the boat.

Cliff would pick him up at six o'clock, Gloria said. Then she turned on her bare heel and made her way up the hill to her house, which had a view, Stu knew, that went forever.

First thing the kid did was go into the cabin, where, unlike Stu, he could stand up. He played with the gimbaled lamp, which was always level, no matter how the boat tilted. He peered out the portholes. He lifted the lid of the coffin berth and gathered up the dividers, the parallel rule, and the lapboard. Stu found a pencil and an old chart and let the boy draw circles and lines until the chart looked like the desperate calculations of a confused sailor.

When he tired of that, he came out into the cockpit, and Stu let him climb into the captain's seat. He peered up the sandy river and played with the wheel as if he was steering a course as complicated as the one he had drawn on the chart.

Late in the morning, the sun finally made its way into the valley of the Green. Stu rummaged among his lockers for lunch. He wound up with beef stew and peaches. Brian ate very little of what Stu called Stu Stew, but he loved the peaches.

After lunch, Stu climbed over the side of the boat and down to the sandy bottom of the river. He lifted Brian down after him, and they walked around 247, inspecting the bottom, using sand to scrub slime and grit from the topsides. In the weeks he had been there, the boat was already cleaner than it had been in years.

Late in the afternoon, they saw the little rafts of sand grains floating in the pools. They got down on their knees to inspect. It was the first sign of the rise. Brian poked a raft with his finger and the grains separated and sank through the water like snow globe glitter.

It took a few minutes for the water to rise a foot and turn gray. Stu lifted Brian back into the boat and then climbed in after him. The river continued to rise, and soon 247 began to bump the bottom, like a horse pawing. Finally, it floated free, and water dripped from the ropes as they stretched against the force of the current.

Brian ran from side to side, laughing at the way the boat rocked.

Stu stayed in the captain's seat and kept a watch. You never knew what new drift logs the daily release from Aldair Dam would pick up and use for battering rams that day.

Stu waited for the river to finish rising. When it was four feet deep and running fast and grey and filling the channel from bank to bank, and when all the debris that always came with the rise had washed past them, Stu asked the boy what time he thought it was.

"Fissshh," the boy said.

Stu opened the cockpit locker and took out their poles. Brian's was a stick, whittled white and curved like a scimitar. Stu baited his own hook and tossed his line over the side. Then he offered to bait Brian's, but the boy shook his head. He dug in the empty peach can and pulled out an imaginary worm, which he inched onto an imaginary hook. Then he threw his thin, imaginary line over the side and they fished.

Stu got nibbles, but Brian got bites. His rod jerked, and he pulled back, hooking fish that threatened to yank him over. Stu put his rod down many times and held Brian by the waist as he fought giant fish. When the monsters emerged from the water, Brian fell back onto the deck with them, and they both flopped around until Brian managed to secure the fish in a bear hug and throw it overboard again.

"You are the man," Stu said after one such struggle, "when it comes to giant imaginaries."

Brian beamed. He re-baited and threw his invisible hook over the side again. The current flowed past, always pulling at them, but 247 held steady.

The sun was about to set behind the hills when there was a disturbance in the laurel. Gravel and stones cascaded down the path. Cliff emerged from the leaves, wearing a white shirt, dark pants, and wingtips. His sleeves were rolled up and his collar was open. He looked up and nodded at Stu.

"What's he doing?" Cliff said, pointing at the boy with his chin.

"Fishing," Stu said, drawing out the "sh" the way the kid did.

"What with?" Cliff said.

The boy bowed his head.

Stu shrugged.

"Supposed to be a difference between fishing and staring at the water like an idiot," Cliff said.

"It's just play," said Stu.

"Oh, please," Cliff said. "Why don't you put a hook and line on that pole, Brian? Afraid of fish?"

Brian hunched his shoulders. His pole balanced on the gunwale for a moment before it clattered to the deck. Stu looked over at him, but the kid was empty as an old can.

"I've been researching this navigable stream nonsense," Cliff said to Stu. "And you're going to have to leave."

What a revelation it had been when Stu learned that no one could own navigable streams. You could drop anchor anywhere, and no one could say a word. Stu had never in his life had a place to call his own, but now he could call an infinite number of places his. And no one, no matter how rich, could do a legal thing about it.

"That's right," Cliff said. "Most of the time there's not enough water here to float a toy boat. That makes it non-navigable. And that means you're trespassing, and wonderful as your visit has been, we will be saying goodbye to you very soon."

Stu smiled. He did not want conflict with this man, his daughter's husband, his grandson's father. "This is a boat," he said. "I got here by water."

"And these ropes," Cliff said, "they can't be tied to my trees. They've got to be below the high water mark."

Stu kept his smile hanging out front, but he backed away from it inside. He reeled in his hook and set his pole down. Then he pulled the line and brought 247 up close to the bank. He told Brian it was time to go home, and he lifted him over the gunwale and handed him off.

Cliff set him down immediately. Then he turned away without a word and headed up the path.

Brian waited.

"I'll see you tomorrow," Stu said.

"Brian!" Cliff shouted.

The boy turned and disappeared up into the laurel.

*   *   *

Stu was in the captain's chair drinking coffee the next morning when Gloria showed up. 247 sat more awkwardly than ever. Its bow nosed into a hole still full of clear green water but the stern angled upward on a sandbar. The boat seemed frozen in a precarious moment just before the wave hits, just before the hull cracks.

Gloria stepped from the laurel and looked down at him, droplets of dew in her dark hair. "Cliff took him," she said, "to preschool."

The tilt of Stu's chair leaned him back too far like at the dentist. "But," he said.

"Brian hates it," Gloria said, "*hates* it. But Cliff wins. Either he wins or he's pissed."

Stu fought his way out of the chair and struggled to stand on the slanted deck. "What's he got to win about?"

"Look," Gloria said. "Brian talks to you, but so what? What good's it do? He won't talk to anybody else, so it's just trouble. Do us all a favor and go, okay? It's what you'll do anyway, so just get it over with."

Stu leaned there looking at his daughter. "I was gone," he admitted, "but it was your mom who left."

Gloria nodded. "Gone would be good."

*   *   *

The day passed slowly without Brian. Lunch was beets and tuna fish, which turned out to be not so bad. Stu lay on his berth in the deep shade beneath the archway of trees and listened to the jungle cries of pileated woodpeckers. Drifty, Stu thought, as he lay there waiting for the rise. He was lazy with waiting, but his mother would have said God was the word he was looking for.

Breezes disturbed the leaves. The water murmured. He heard the plop of, perhaps, muskrats, and the shush of sand against the hull as if 247 was making its way in low water, parting sand like a plow. Great drifts of it piled up on either side of 247 and the boat began to sink into the sand, a sunken thing sinking even farther. That was when he realized he had been sleeping.

He put his face to the porthole and saw lightning flashes outlining the hills to the west. In a groggy panic, he stumbled into the cockpit expecting the boat to be adrift on the storm-swollen river, the lines cut, its bottom dragging, tortured, across the sand.

Stu looked over the side and saw that the river was not deep enough to float 247 yet. But there was the boy standing in water up to his knees. His hands were full of sand and he was scrubbing 247's hull. The river was already moving fast enough to wash sand out from beneath the kid's feet so that he did a little dance, shifting his footing constantly.

The kid yelped when Stu leaned over the side and grabbed the back of his shirt. But when Stu set him on the work deck and knelt down in front of him, the kid blinked and smiled, happy as a mortal lifted into heaven.

Stu could not find words. How did the boy get there? Had he run away? Was it that bad at home? Should Stu take him back? Should he keep him there?

The boy said, "Fish."

"Yeah?" Stu said. "You okay? You just wanna play?"

Stu looked toward the hill for Gloria or Cliff, but he heard gravel cascade into the water from the other side of the river. He turned around in time to see her sliding down the bank on her rear end. She plopped into the river and was on her feet in a flash. The water was up to her thighs, and she turned sideways to the current so she could edge out into the deeper water toward the boat. When she was in up to her waist, she lost her footing, and Stu barely caught her hand before the current carried her out of reach. He dropped a looped line over the side, and once she was able to get her foot in it, he managed to tumble her on board.

They lay on the deck, side by side, panting.

"Fish!" Brian said.

She sat up. Her shirt clung to her body, and a puddle grew beneath her. "You talked," she said. "He talked!"

Stu had thought it was Gloria—the dark hair, the long neck. But it was JoAnna. She was smiling, amazed. He could not remember the last time he had seen her happy in his presence.

The boy ran from one side of the cockpit to the other. "Seeit?" he said. "Seeit?"

JoAnna stood up but did a little stutter-step because of the rocking. "Yes," she said, but Brian was already in the cabin where he pointed to the gimbaled lamp, motionless as a gyroscope. "See?"

She stopped at the hatchway and looked back at Stu. "He talks around you?" she said.

"Some," Stu said.

"Well," she said. "Aren't you special."

Stu smiled. He had not been special since he was seven or eight and his mother told the neighbors that for a dollar a seventh son could stand up to God and heal.

JoAnna leaned over and tried to wring water out of her cuffs. "I never would have let him go down there if I knew the water came up so fast," she said. "Scared me to death." She pointed to her side of the river, twenty feet away. "Can you take us back?"

It was already getting dark. Thunder boomed from the mountains, and the river had risen much higher than usual, going beyond grey to a yellow-brown, thick with mud and debris.

Stu went to the wheel. He hit the start button, and the diesel caught cylinder by cylinder until a sound like a bulldozer drowned out the thunder. He untied the lines from Cliff's trees. Back at the wheel, he put the boat in gear and moved forward against the current.

He angled toward JoAnna's side of the river and felt the power in his hands. The bow touched the bank, and Stu gave 247 more throttle to keep it planted there. He went forward then and shined the spotlight. Water was already over the bank on that side, running who knew how deep another fifty feet inland.

Stu went back to the cockpit and dug out the life jackets. By the time JoAnna and Brian were jacketed and they all got up front again, the flooded ground stretched out farther than before, and JoAnna would not even consider leaving the boat.

They all trooped back to the cockpit. Stu pulled back to his old spot and tied off to Cliff's trees again.

"Well," he said, after he had shut the diesel down.

"Well," JoAnna said.

They took off their life jackets and looked at each other.

"I guess we stay until the water goes down," Stu said.

"And that is when?" she said.

"Three, four in the morning, usually," he told her. "But storms can change everything."

"Gloria wanted him to stay at my house," JoAnna said. "She wanted to keep him away from Cliff. She's coming to get him in the morning—at eight."

Stu nodded. Then he raised his eyebrows and shrugged.

"Shit," JoAnna breathed. "She told me not to bring him down here."

Stu invited her into the cabin to get dry clothes. They had to hunch over and stand so close that they could not avoid touching. It made him feel for moments as if they were married again, their lives all stirred into each other. Stu dug fresh jeans and a blue shirt from under his berth. "Come on, young man," he said to Brian. "Let's give your grandmother some privacy."

JoAnna came out of the cabin in a few minutes holding Stu's jeans up by a belt loop. "I need something," she announced.

Stu found a piece of line the right length, and JoAnna wrapped it twice around her waist and knotted it. Then she raised her arms. "How do I look?"

"Fine," Stu said. She looked like a girl to him, somehow, a girl in familiar clothes. "How do you feel?"

She shook her head and looked around as if able to take things in for the first time. "This is a huge boat."

Stu nodded.

"Gloria said you were living down here, but I didn't believe it. I mean, 'living in what,' I said, 'a row boat?' But this is amazing. How'd you get it here?"

"Diesel fuel," he said, "and lots of cussing."

The wind picked up and rain began to fall. They took refuge in the cabin. Lightning strobed in the woods, making shadow-mantises and stick-crickets of the trees.

Stu lit the lamp. It hung unperturbed in its gimbaled mount while 247 bucked and shied. Shadows convulsed through the cabin. JoAnna sat on the berth with her arm around the boy. Light from the lamp hooded their eyes in shadow.

Drift logs boomed into the bow from time to time, and unidentified things scraped and screeched along the sides of the hull. Everything pitched and bobbed, tilted and tipped, everything, except the lamp, which Stu watched, stilling himself.

"How about dinner?" he said.

JoAnna looked at him doubtfully.

He opened a locker filled with rusty, unlabeled cans. "I've got meat, vegetables, and fruit."

"Peaches," said Brian.

Stu lifted cans from the locker one at a time and shook. The three he picked turned out to be ravioli, diced carrots, and, yes, more peaches. The ravioli and carrots went into pots, and when the boat was momentarily still, Stu lit the stove and clamped the pots in place. The cabin seemed to grow warmer and larger as the smells filled it. Stu suggested they all sit knee to knee on the floor where the boat's motion would be less pronounced. He put the pots on the floor between them and gave everyone a fork.

Brian stabbed a ravioli. "Fisssh," he said and slid it into his mouth.

By the time they had finished eating, it was almost as if they no longer noticed the motion of the boat. Stu took his rain gear from the peg and got ready to check the lines. He paused at the hatch and looked back into the cabin.

JoAnna and Brian lifted their faces and light streamed into the caves that had been their eyes. JoAnna tried to get Brian to say, "Thank you, Granddad." But the boy would not.

*   *   *

The river writhed between its banks. The lightning had moved off to the east and the wind settled down, but drift logs and debris swung by on the current, booming downstream. The roots of a floating tree snagged one of the lines and the trunk banged against the side of the boat. Stu went forward and pulled with both hands to make slack. Then he whipped the line with all his might so that it lifted over the roots. The tree was suddenly harmless, and it floated away down the river. Stu sat down, straddling the bow and watched the steady stream of things that came down on the current in the light of the lopsided moon—things of people and things of nature, dead things and living things. Snakes and muskrats were out of their holes, bait cans and beer cartons ghosted away from fishing spots, and lots of logs that had waited, half sodden, on the river bank for years had been lifted into the current by the high water, and they ghosted downstream like torpedoes.

Stu heard the hatch open and a yellow glow lit the work deck. JoAnna walked to the stern, pots in hand, and bent over to wash them in the river.

He thought at first that the back and forth of the boat made a tree stump on JoAnna's side of the river appear to move. But really it did move, a step or two at a time, along the edge of the water, which was still flowing over the bank. It paced in the woods, just a silhouette, hands in its pockets, cowboy hat pulled low against the night. Then it called JoAnna's name.

She did not look up.

The silhouette put a hand to its forehead. It walked, ankle deep into the water. Then the hands went into its pockets and came out again. It wanted to know what JoAnna thought she was doing. It wanted to know why had she come down there anyway, and when was she coming home, and where was the kid, by the way, and, really, how long was this going to go on, and, furthermore, Jesus H. Christ!

JoAnna murmured something. Stu remembered how she had stopped talking in the weeks before she took Gloria and left him. It hadn't been the silent treatment with all its hope of repentance. No, it was just that she had nothing more to say. She was done. And then she and Gloria were gone and it was years before Stu managed to pry his way back into their lives, years that had cost him his relationship with his daughter.

The silhouette put its hands back in its pockets and paced a few more steps. Then, quickly as it came, it turned and merged back into the trees.

Stu made his way to the stern where Joanna stood, both hands on the transom, looking downstream at the muddy current zooming away.

"Brian's asleep, I think."

"Good," Stu said.

"We thought something was wrong with him," she said. "We did. I mean autism, something. The tests didn't show it, but who knew? Something was not right." She turned toward him. The distant lamp cast a pale yellow light on her like a tin-type. "Down here, though, with you . . . Do you know he said 'good night,' to me just now? My god, Stu, he's a boy down here. A regular boy." She looked sideways at him.

"Diesel fuel," Stu said. "Lots of cussing."

"Seriously."

Stu shook his head. What could he say? They had just seemed to click, somehow. "Who was that on the bank?" he said.

"My soon-to-be ex," she said. "He hasn't figured out how to ex yet."

Stu didn't trust this woman. When had there ever been reason to trust her? She was the unattainable. He had reached for her and missed. She was never satisfied with Stu. Stu who married her even though she was pregnant. No, Stu was only the best she was able to do at that desperate time. Once the trouble passed, she needed more and better bests. It had always been that way for JoAnna. And now Ken was finding it out too.

Stu excused himself and went forward to the bow. A log had

caught on a line, and Stu had felt the vibrations. He shoved the log with the boathook and it swung off the line and thumped 247's bow before screeching its way down the side.

By the time he got back to the stern, the log had disappeared into the darkness downstream, and JoAnna was gone, too. Stu saw the light in the cabin go out. She would want to rise early to get the kid back before Gloria came for him. What a mess, Stu thought. He put the hood up on his rain gear. The night was damp and cool. The woods dripped.

He dozed in the captain's chair, still aware, at some level, of the sound and feel of the boat in the current. Three times during the night, he went forward to clear the line. The third time it was almost dawn. A knobby, wooden thing, polished smooth as a skull, had caught there, bobbing and nodding in the current.

Stu sat on the bow and watched. The current came at him from the darkness under the trees, and the knob nodded in the flow like an idiot agreeing with something it could never understand. He should push it off but it was hypnotic. He leaned back against the front of the cabin.

When she touched his shoulder, he opened his eyes to see her smiling down. "Been up all night?"

"Some of it," he confessed.

She shivered and put her arms around herself. Her eyes were puffy. The morning was grey.

She sat next to him and he draped his jacket over her shoulders. They leaned back against the cabin to watch the water come at them from the gloom of earliest morning. Mist drifted in the eddies, but the morning gave no hint about what sort of day lay ahead. The sun might cut through the mist and make a bright blue day, or the grey could easily deepen into rain.

They could get to shore now, he told her. The river was still high but back inside its banks.

"He's asleep," she said.

Stu nodded. He stared forward at the current. The knob that had snagged on the line bobbed. In spite of all the years he had spent imagining a moment like this alone with his ex, he found now that he did not have a thing to say.

The water grew brighter as the sky broke into blue beyond the canopy of leaves, and Gloria seemed to materialize with the morning, framed between sycamores where the path that led from JoAnna's house opened to the river. Stu saw that she was watching them, and he felt himself freeze, like prey. JoAnna stiffened. Slowly, casually, she pulled away from Stu and sat up straighter.

Gloria stepped forward. "Where is he?" she said.

"The high water just caught us," JoAnna said. "I didn't even know what was happening, and then here we were. Didn't even have my phone with me."

Gloria glared at Stu. Clearly, he was still a screw-up.

JoAnna ducked into the cabin to wake Brian, but Stu could tell he was already awake by how quickly he got cranky. He screamed at his grandmother, and she came out a moment later with Brian wrapped in Stu's blanket. The boy worked his hands free and wiped his eyes. JoAnna set him on his feet in the cockpit. He scowled across the water at his mother.

"Alright," Gloria said. "How do we do this? I've got places to be."

Stu said he would start the diesel and power the bow into the bank so the boy could hop off. But before he could even reach the starter button, the boy had shed the blanket and hopped on top of the cabin. He scrambled up the diesel stack and then climbed off into the tree limbs above the boat, where he hung, upside down like a possum.

"Brian," his mother said, "cut it out!"

The boy made his way along the branch until he got to a fork and could turn upright. He grinned back across the river, then at the boat and Gloria beyond.

"I'm going to call your father," Gloria said. "He'll come down and get you."

The boy's lips pulled back off his teeth, his neck corded, and his fingers went white around the branches. He screamed at them—incoherent and grotesque, a boy become an animal.

Gloria took out her phone and began to dial.

The animal in the tree went berserk. He shook the branches. He howled. He hit his head against the limbs.

Gloria made the call and then flipped the phone shut. "You're going to get it now," she said.

Eyes and mouth round, Brian climbed back out above the boat. He looked down at Gloria on the bank and then to Stu and JoAnna.

"Come on, honey," JoAnna said and held out her arms. The boy climbed down into them and huddled against her. Stu draped his blanket over Brian's shoulders.

"Now," Gloria said, "can we try this again?"

The boy rocked in JoAnna's arms.

The disturbance in the laurel revealed itself to be Cliff coming down his side of the river. He ducked from the leaves and stepped to the riverside dressed in a suit and tie. His hands went to his hips.

"He wouldn't come," Gloria said. "He was on that side of the river, but then he climbed back out. And now there he is."

Cliff rolled his eyes along the arc of branches that hung above the boat. He shook his head.

Stu sat there in the captain's seat swiveling his attention from JoAnna's side of the river, where Gloria stood to Cliff's side. Everybody, he thought, should just back off and give the kid some space, some quiet.

"Boy!" Cliff said. "Get over there to your mother." He turned toward Stu. "Get that boat over there and let him off."

The river was falling, the water slowly going a greener grey, but Stu could still get 247 to the bank if he wanted. He had powered through shallows like this before.

"Too shallow," he told Cliff.

"Are you kidding?" Gloria said. "You didn't get that boat fifty miles farther upstream than it ought to go by not being able to get to the goddamn shore."

"In a little while," Stu said, "you'll be able to walk out here."

'I've got to get to work," Cliff said, and Gloria complained that she was already late.

Stu shrugged and said he didn't control the river.

"Jesus Christ!" Cliff said, "Why is it that all the crap winds up in the river?"

"Maybe," JoAnna said, "we shouldn't go to school today. Maybe we should stay here until the water goes down. You two go on. I'll take care of him."

"That's *my* son," Cliff said.

JoAnna turned around and faced him, silent.

Cliff's scowl fell apart. "We'll just see about this," he said. Then he ducked back into the laurel and made his way up the hill.

Gloria watched the disturbance rise. Then she turned to JoAnna. "Do you have any idea what this is going to do? Do you know the hell he'll put us through thanks to you?"

"And you," she pointed to Stu, "make nothing but trouble." She shot a hard look at Brian and then she turned from the river and set out across the wide bottomland that led to JoAnna's house.

It was always like this. The more things Stu tried to fix the more broken they seemed to get.

JoAnna stood at the gunwale and watched Gloria disappear. "I just wanted the best for her," she said. "You know? And I was right. He was it. She's got a bigger house than I do and a richer husband, too. She has it all. But turns out she doesn't think I make much of a god."

"Who does?" Stu said. He watched the current pushing past. The world just kept coming at you. You could try to fend it off for a while, but it wouldn't stop. And what were you supposed to do with what it brought?

Gloria had not let her mother run everything. She had kept her heart for herself and had a child with the boy she loved. He was not Cliff's son. There was not a bit of Cliff in the boy.

JoAnn asked if he would pull into the mouth of a small stream that flowed through her property. Stu started the diesel and nosed half the boat's length into the ravine. It fit snug as a slip.

JoAnna collected her wet clothes and grabbed the boy's hand. She stood with him on the gunwale and they stepped together off the boat and onto dry land. "Thank you," she said to Stu.

Stu looked at her and nodded.

"You can tie to my trees if you want," she said. "Might save trouble, you know, with the other side."

"Yours?"

"In a few weeks they'll be mine."

"I don't know what to do," Stu admitted.

"Who does?" she said. She put her arm around the boy and told him to say "Bye, Granddad," but he would not.

She shrugged and smiled, and then she and the boy turned and headed up the path that led to JoAnna's house.

He watched them walk away. The best thing would be for Stu to leave before he mattered. He was just a guy in a big boat now. The kid might remember a thing or two, but Stu would fade.

There was enough water in the river, and now that 247 was nosed into JoAnna's creek, there was room to turn the boat around. He could get miles downstream before he would have to lay up for the next rise. He could head back to the tide and be nothing but a vague old man.

The boy stopped on the path and looked back. JoAnna stopped and turned.

The boy lifted his hand. "Gandy," he shouted. "Gandy!"

JoAnna waved, too, and they disappeared around the bend.

All he had to do was pull the lever into reverse and back out down the river, but he shoved the shifter forward and opened the throttle. The prop threw mud and water and pushed the boat almost all the way into the ravine. The back would float at high water but the bow would always be in mud. And with the fiberglass worn away, the worms would go to work on the wood. There was enough diesel for weeks of keeping the batteries charged and the pump working, but once that was gone the boat would fill with water and mud. After a couple big rains, the hull would begin to come apart, and things would go fast after that. A few more storms and 247 would be only a scattering of stuff on the bottom: rusted steel, rotting plywood, screws and nails and pieces of glass blasted by sand.

No, the boat was doomed, but "Gandy" blossomed in him like a smile. He had decisions to make. He knew secrets, now, and he had the happiness of other people in his hands.

When time came, he thought, he would know what to do.

Acknowledgments ─────────────────────────────────

Many people helped make this book possible. My thanks to New Rivers Press, Alan Davis, Nathan Rundquist, and the book team: Taylor Brown, Sheena Norstedt, Morgan Tuscherer, and Sarah Bosak.

Thanks also goes to my old friends Rodney Weaver and David Dodd, who showed me the power of voice and living stories. Thanks to Dabney Townsend, who turned on my literary lights, and to novelist William Wiser—friend, mentor, model.

Thanks to Morningside College, whose support, encouragement, and patience have been sustaining forces for me. And, most importantly, thanks to my long-time writing group: Nancy Braun, Tricia Currans-Sheehan, Jeanne Emmons, Deb Freese, Barb Gross, and Marlene Vander Weil--what insightful and useful readers. Thanks, also to my children, Andrew and Laura, for keeping me in touch with the raw nerve-ends of life. And thanks to my wife, Lynne—supporter, inspiration, critic, and fan. And to all my friends: I could never have done it without you.

Finally, thanks to the following publications for giving these stories their first lives:

"Edna and Coy" (published as "Hunting Country"). *The Southern Review*, 2000. Republished in *New Stories from the South*, 2001. Republished in *Best of the South II*, Algonquin Books, 2005.

"Hollowed Be Thy Name." *The North American Review*, Volume 289, Number 2, March-April, 2004.

"The Grease Man." *Prairie Schooner*, Volume 64, Number 1, Spring 1990.

"How Love Feels." *The North American Review*, Volume 296, Number 2. Spring 2011.

"Ice Boy." *New Millennium Writings*, Number 23, 2014.

"JoAnna's Story" (published as "Jill's Story"). *The North American Review*, Volume 292, Number 2, March-April 2007.

"The Mercy of the World." *The New England Review*, Volume 28, Number 2, 2007.

"M.I.A." (published as "Missing in Action"). *The Georgia Review*, Volume L, Number 4, December 1996.

"Salvage." *American Short Fiction*. Volume 5, Number 20, December 1995.

"Still Life." *The South Carolina Review*, Volume 40, Number 1, Fall, 2007.

"Stu's Story" (published as "Everything Important Makes No Sense"). *The Robert's Writing Awards Annual*, 1991.

"The Visitation." *The North American Review*, Volume 286, Numbers 3-4. May-August, 2001.

"Waiting Room" (published as "The Long Room"). *The Greensboro Review*, Number 72, Fall 2002.

About the Author _____

Stephen Coyne grew up fishing and trapping in the swamps of the Delaware and Chesapeake bays. As a boy, the watermen who plied the shallows and harvested a muddy abundance fascinated him, and one of his earliest goals was to live on a boat. He has done factory work, welding, carpentry, boatwrighting, and teaching for a living. He has labored happily in junkyards, boatyards, auto shops, body shops, and writing workshops. Like Whitman, he has enjoyed separate circles of friends—the folks and the freaks—the people and the artists who think about them.

His novel in stories, *It Turns Out Like This*, won the Many Voices Award from New Rivers Press. His short stories and poems have appeared in *The Southern Review, The Georgia Review, The New England Review, The North American Review, Prairie Schooner*, and elsewhere. He has won a *Playboy Magazine* College Fiction prize, a Robert's Writing Award, a Heartland Fiction Prize, and a *Prairie Schooner* Reader's Choice Award. His story, "Hunting Country," was chosen by Ann Tyler as one of the best stories published about the South from 1996 to 2006 and is republished in *Best of the South II* from Algonquin Books. His story "Iceboy" won the 2013 *New Millennium Prize* for Fiction. Coyne teaches American literature and creative writing at Morningside College, in Sioux City, Iowa.

About New Rivers Press

New Rivers Press emerged from a drafty Massachusetts barn in winter 1968. Intent on publishing work by new and emerging poets, founder C. W. "Bill" Truesdale labored for weeks over an old Chandler & Price letterpress to publish three hundred fifty copies of Margaret Randall's collection, So Many Rooms Has a House But One Roof.

Nearly four hundred titles later, New Rivers, a non-profit and now teaching press based since 2001 at Minnesota State University Moorhead, has remained true to Bill's goal of publishing the best new literature—poetry and prose—from new, emerging, and established writers.

New Rivers Press authors range in age from twenty to eighty-nine. They include a silversmith, a carpenter, a geneticist, a monk, a tree-trimmer, and a rock musician. They hail from cities such as Christchurch, Honolulu, New Orleans, New York City, Northfield (Minnesota), and Prague.

Charles Baxter, one of the first authors with New Rivers, calls the press "the hidden backbone of the American literary tradition." Continuing this tradition, in 1981 New Rivers began to sponsor the Minnesota Voices Project (now called Many Voices Project) competition. It is one of the oldest literary competitions in the United States, bringing recognition and attention to emerging writers. Other New Rivers publications include the American Fiction Series, the American Poetry Series, New Rivers Abroad, and the Electronic Book Series.

Please visit our website
newriverspress.com for more information.

Many Voices Project Award Winners ──────────

"OP" indicates that the paper copy is out of print;
"e-book" indicates that the title is available as an electronic publication.

#134   It Turns Out Like This, *Stephen Coyne (e-book)*
#133   A Beautiful Hell, *Carol Kapaun Ratchenski*
#132   Home Studies, *Julie Gard (e-book)*
#131   Flashcards & The Curse of Ambrosia, *Tracy Robert (e-book)*
#130   Dispensations, *Randolph Thomas (e-book)*
#129   Invasives, *Brandon Krieg*
#128   Whitney, *Joe Stracci (e-book)*
#127   Rare Earth, *Bradford Tice*
#126   The Way of All Flux, *Sharon Suzuki-Martinez*
#125   It Takes You Over, *Nick Healy (e-book)*
#124   The Muse of Ocean Parkway and Other Stories,
         Jacob Lampart (e-book)
#123   Hotel Utopia, *Robert Miltner*
#122   Kinesthesia, *Stephanie N. Johnson*
#121   Birds of Wisconsin, *B.J. Best*
#120   At Home Anywhere, *Mary Hoffman (e-book)*
#119   Friend Among Stones, *Maya Pindyck*
#118   Fallibility, *Elizabeth Oness*
#117   When Love Was Clean Underwear, *Susan Barr-Toman (e-book)*
#116   The Sound of It, *Tim Nolan*
#115   Hollow Out, *Kelsea Habecker*
#114   Bend from the Knees, *Benjamin Drevlow*
#113   The Tender, Wild Things, *Diane Jarvenpa*
#112   Signaling for Rescue, *Marianne Herrmann*
#111   Cars Go Fast, *John Chattin*
#110   Terrain Tracks, *Purvi Shah*
#109   Numerology and Other Stories, *Christian Michener*